Ten Seconds To Play!

The Chip Hilton Sports Series

For more information on
Chip Hilton-related activities and to correspond
with other Chip fans, check the Internet at
chiphilton.com

Chip Hilton Sports Series
#12

Ten Seconds To Play!

Coach Clair Bee
Updated by Randall and Cynthia Bee Farley
Foreword by Dean E. Smith

BROADMAN
&HOLMAN
PUBLISHERS

Nashville, Tennessee

0-8054-1994-2

Published by Broadman & Holman Publishers,
Nashville, Tennessee
Page Design: Anderson Thomas Design, Nashville, Tennessee
Typesetting: PerfecType, Nashville, Tennessee

Subject Heading: FOOTBALL—FICTION / YOUTH
Library of Congress Card Catalog Number: 99-39092

Library of Congress Cataloging-in-Publication Data
Bee, Clair.
  Ten seconds to play! / Clair Bee ; [edited by Randall and
Cynthia Bee Farley].
    p. cm. — (Chip Hilton sports series; v. 12)
  Updated ed. of work published in 1955.
  Summary: Chip takes a job at a summer camp and
meets a talented athlete who may be joining him on the
football team at State University, and whose arrogance
hides a secret problem.
  ISBN 0-8054-1994-2
  [1. Camps Fiction. 2. Fear Fiction. 3. Football Fiction.]
I. Farley, Randall K., 1952– . II. Farley, Cynthia Bee, 1952– .
III. Title. IV. Series: Bee, Clair. Chip Hilton sports series ;
v. 12.
PZ7.B381955Te 1999
[Fic]—dc21   99-39092
                      CIP

1 2 3 4 5 03 02 01 00 99

TO
NELSON DINGLEY III

COACH CLAIR BEE
1955

TO
STEVE AND EDNA SMITH

The energized, ever-ready world travelers
from North Carolina who
are always there for us and Chip.

LOVE,
RANDY AND CINDY
SUMMER 1999

Contents

CONTENTS

Foreword

WHEN I was ten or eleven years old, I was forced to read books by my parents. Since I liked athletes, I read and enjoyed several books by John R. Tunis that dealt primarily with baseball but also sportsmanship. Now fast forward to the summer of 1959, when at long last I had the opportunity to meet acclaimed basketball coach Clair Bee.

Frank McGuire was a close friend of Coach Bee, and I had just finished my first year as an assistant to Coach McGuire at North Carolina. Coach Bee was helping Frank with his basketball books, *Offensive Basketball* and *Defensive Basketball*. They had asked me to select two topics for chapters in *Defensive Basketball,* so we spent a great deal of time together that summer at the New York Military Academy.

During this period, not only did I stare at the painting of the fictional folk hero—Chip Hilton—that was on the wall behind Coach Bee's dining room table, but I had the opportunity to read some of the Chip Hilton series. The books were extremely interesting and well written, using sports as a vehicle to build character. No one did that better than Clair Bee (although Tunis came close). By that time, Bee's Chip Hilton books had become a classic series for youngsters. While Coach Bee was well known as one of the great coaches of all time due to his strategy and competitiveness, I believe he thought he could help society and young people most by writing this series. In his eyes, it was his "calling" in the years following his college and professional coaching career.

Coach McGuire and I, along with countless other basketball coaches, learned basketball from Clair Bee. The point zone, which Coach Bob Spear and I developed at the Air Force Academy, had its origins in one of Coach Bee's old books on the 1-3-1 rotating zone defense. We made our point zone at Air Force more of a match-up zone, but this is just one instance where people on the basketball court today still depend on innovations by Clair Bee.

From 1959 until his death, I visited with Coach Bee frequently at the New York Military Academy and at Kutsher's Sports Academy, which he directed. He certainly touched my life as a special friend. Not only does he still rank at the top of his profession as a basketball coach, but he now regains the peak as a writer of sports fiction. I am delighted the Chip Hilton sports series has been redone to make it more appropriate for athletics today without losing the deeper meaning of defining character. I encourage everyone to give these books as gifts to other young athletes so that Coach Bee's brilliant method of making sports come to life and building character will continue.

DEAN E. SMITH
Head Coach (Retired), Men's Basketball,
University of North Carolina at Chapel Hill

CHAPTER 1

Camp All-America

THE PURPLE aloofness of the majestic mountains and the spectacular views of the Hudson River valley along the winding Storm King Highway had awed Chip Hilton for the last hour. Chip had seen a number of summer hotels and camps as he peered out the window of the bus, but the view now greeting him was more beautiful than he had dared dream. Beyond the big wooden arch bearing the red-white-and-blue words "CAMP ALL-AMERICA," he glimpsed a broad green lawn and several white buildings surrounded by cottages.

As the bus came to a stop, the panorama of the camp opened up, and Chip's eyes found what they were seeking. On the left of the broad walk was a trim baseball field with a backstop and bleachers. Behind the field was a long row of tennis courts. Over on the right, a six-lane, all-weather track circled a football field. To the right of the gridiron was the basketball area, with six beautiful, full-sized blacktop courts and two courts with eight-foot baskets. Beyond and above the main buildings Chip could see the large Dr. James A. Naismith Field House. Inside, surrounded by bleachers, were three basketball courts that could also serve as tennis courts. Several small offices inside the field house looked out on Bailey Lake.

"Here you are," the bus driver announced. He set the brake and preceded Chip down the steps. "I have to get your bags out of the back. I'll just set them over here by the gate. That's where I pile them when the campers arrive. Camp's got a van, and they'll give you a lift with it." He measured Chip critically. "You look like an athlete. You on the staff?"

Chip nodded. "I'm looking forward to it," he said lightly. "I've never worked at a camp before. It sure looks like a great setup."

"Best in the country," the bus driver remarked, glancing at Chip's hair. "That short hair of yours will be corn yellow before you go home. You'll have a great time." He turned back to the bus and paused with one foot on the step. "You'll make good, all right. You've got a good chin."

Chip carried his backpack up the walk, admiring the well-kept lawn and flower beds. As he approached the buildings he got another pleasant surprise. Right at the end of the walk was a modern swimming pool with a diving tower. Several young men around Chip's age were swimming and splashing in the pool. He stopped to watch. The swimmers were noisy with joyous clamor. Then, suddenly, the action and shouting quieted.

"Phil's going to dive!"

"Hey, Whittemore! How about a two-and-a-halfer?"

The object of attention was swiftly and effortlessly climbing the ladder of the diving tower. Every step of the rapid ascent accented the carved muscles of the bronzed young man's arms, legs, and back. He paused on the diving platform for a moment, looking down on his audience with an amused smile.

"Make it a good one, Phil!" someone yelled. "Make it a triple somersault!"

"Why not?" the tanned athlete said rather arrogantly, shrugging his wide shoulders. "Sure, why not?" he repeated as he swaggered forward and posed in the ready position on the board.

Chip evaluated the diver. He was about six-four, well padded with muscle, and carried about 210 pounds. His black curly hair and dark brown eyes were framed above with heavy eyebrows, and Chip figured girls might call him handsome. But the petulant carriage of his heavy lips and his arrogant swagger detracted tremendously from the physical impression.

The diver on the board stood rigid, his arms and hands straight down, as if waiting for the board and the water and his nerves to still, seeking perfect timing for a perfect execution.

Taking two long strides and a slight jump, the lithe figure catapulted high in the air, twirling head over heels twice and then a third time. Ten feet above the water he straightened out and knifed into the pool like a flashing spear. It was almost unbelievable that such a big person could enter the water with so little splash, hardly more than a ripple.

"That was good," Chip murmured.

There was a sudden burst of applause. And when the black curly head emerged from the water, Chip joined in the tribute. The diver's powerful stroke carried him to the side of the pool, and with no apparent effort he pulled himself out of the water and leaped to his feet.

"Terrific, Phil, terrific!"

"Olympic stuff, Whitty. Olympic stuff!"

"You can say that again," Chip murmured in admiration. He picked up his backpack and headed for the building on the left, where he could see a group of adults standing on the porch. As he approached, a tall, broad-shouldered man detached himself from the group and met him with an outstretched hand.

"You must be Chip Hilton." The big man smiled in welcome. "I'm Frank Dodd." He gripped Chip's hand and shook it vigorously. "I'd know you anywhere, Hilton. I saw you play freshman ball at State. In fact, I was so impressed that I begged Curly Ralston to have you work up here for the summer. You probably don't know it, but I played a little football at State a few years back myself. C'mon. Meet the rest of the folks."

Frank Dodd would have been surprised, but Chip Hilton knew all about his football prowess at State. Curly Ralston, State's head football coach, had told Chip he was going to be working for one of State's most fervent alumni football fanatics. "He probably talks football in his sleep," Ralston had warned Chip the day Rockwell suggested the job at Camp All-America.

"Rock" had been Chip's coach, mentor, and friend all through Valley Falls High School and also during his first year at State. "You'll earn some money and have a chance to keep in condition, Chip, but more important," Rockwell had said, "you'll have a chance to work with kids. And I know of no better way to spend a summer," Rockwell had reflected a moment before continuing softly, "or a lifetime."

That was enough for Chip. Rock thought it was the right thing for him to do, and Mary Hilton, Chip's mom, always seconded Henry Rockwell's guidance. So here he was! And, so far, he liked it.

"Chip, this is Mrs. Dodd. Deana, meet Chip Hilton."

Mrs. Dodd smiled warmly. She was small and compactly built, and her handshake was firm. Chip liked her friendly manner. Then Dodd introduced Cliff Burdette and Joel Goldstein, explaining that Burdette was camp director and Goldstein was in charge of the waterfront and all swimming activities. Burdette was small, wiry, and intense in manner. He moved with quick motions, and his speech was rapid but friendly. Goldstein was short and broad. *Mr. Five-by-Five,* Chip was thinking as he shook hands with the powerful man.

"Bill Smith is in charge of athletics, Chip. You'll work with him this summer. He's around somewhere. By the way, how's State going to shape up this fall?"

Without giving Chip a chance to reply, Dodd continued enthusiastically, "Oughta be terrific. Starting backfield will be back intact. I guess you know them all: Ace Gibbons, Boots Cole, Buzz Burk and . . ." He paused and flashed a knowing wink. "And, of course, Tims Lansing. You're probably not worrying too much about him though. After watching you quarterback last year—"

Deana Dodd placed a hand on her husband's arm. "Frank," she remonstrated, "Chip's tired after his long trip. Let him have a few moments to relax and unwind. Besides, you'll have all summer to talk football."

Cliff Burdette chuckled. "No doubt about that," he added dryly.

From the direction of the pool came a burst of applause. Dodd turned to Chip. "That's for Whitty," he said proudly. "He's a terrific athlete; good at everything. He plays any game. It comes easy to him. He's been with me for years; started here as a camper, and I've been coaching him ever since. He's on the staff now.

"Important thing is, he's one of the greatest college football players I've ever seen." He nudged Chip in the ribs, "present company excluded, of course. And," Dodd continued, "he's going to State this fall. Ralston's counting on him to start. He plays at either end of the line and pulls in a pass like Alex Rodriguez pulls in a baseball."

Chip was puzzled. "Transfers can't play, can they, Mr. Dodd?"

"He's not transferring, Chip. Whitty graduated from Central Junior College last week. He's eligible to play right away—this September. Come on, I'll introduce you."

"Frank!" Deana Dodd interrupted. "You promised! Remember?" She turned to Goldstein. "Joel, help Chip get settled, will you, please?"

Despite Chip's protests, Joel Goldstein picked up his backpack and led the way. "We've got a few guys on staff who aren't football players, Chip," he said dryly. "I'll see that you meet them. Right now, I want to give you a little history on Camp All-America."

Chip appreciated the kindness behind Goldstein's words. Joel spouted information like an auctioneer and told him all about Camp All-America. This man obviously loved his work and the camp with all his heart. Chip learned that Dodd, Goldstein, Burdette, and Bill Smith had been classmates at State and had all joined in making All-America the most outstanding camp in New York State. Although Goldstein, Burdette, and Smith were salaried employees, Dodd, the actual owner of the camp, regarded them as partners.

"You'll like Bill Smith, Chip. He's a great guy. Confidentially, Bill is the only one of the four of us who was a top athlete. He lettered every year in football. He's still in good shape.

"Oh, by the way, Frank was also a running back and did a few plays as a receiver. Mostly, he played behind Bill. He'll try to convince you he's the greatest line buster since Emmitt Smith and the best receiver since Jerry Rice. On top of that, he thinks he's a coach. But it's all in fun. You'll find him one of the greatest guys you'll ever meet. You met Deana, his wife. Salt of the earth, the real boss of the camp. And the kids, Frank Jr. and Jimmie, well, you'll meet them soon enough. Too soon!"

Chip was saved by the camp loudspeaker announcing dinner. But that didn't stop Joel Goldstein. He table-hopped Chip all over the dining room, introducing him to everyone in sight. Then he led him to a table where a man was sitting alone. "This is your boss, Chip. Bill Smith. Bill, this is Chip Hilton."

Smith greeted Chip warmly. "Sit down, Chip. This is our table, and your regular place will be here on my right. I heard Joel had you making the rounds. How do you like Camp All-America?"

Chip enjoyed the conversation not only because he found his boss a friendly, understanding person, but also because he learned a great deal about his job. Smith was all business and never once referred to football or State athletics.

"We're having a staff meeting tonight, Chip," Smith said, as they rose from the table. "Eight o'clock in the little theater. We're going to show a camp video from last year. It'll give you a better idea of our program than a week of talking. Uh oh," he said, grinning. "Here comes Frank, and he's got Whitty in tow. You're in for some football talk."

Chip had known all along that Whitty would be the diver he had watched. He smiled pleasantly as Frank Dodd guided the tall swimmer forward for the introduction.

"Whitty, this is Chip Hilton. Chip, meet Philip Whittemore."

Whittemore gave Chip a steady, almost insolent stare and then grasped Chip's extended hand with a hard, tough grip, going all out in an effort to demonstrate his tremendous strength. Chip tightened his own grip to meet the pressure, giving as good as he got, recognizing Whittemore's desire for domination. It was a brief, tense moment, and Chip could almost feel the intense antagonism Whittemore expressed through the less than cordial handshake. Then the big diver loosened his grip and turned abruptly away.

"Did you want me for something, Frank?"

Dodd nodded emphatically. "Sure, Whitty. I wanted the best pass receiver in the country to meet the greatest quarterback in the business. You two players are going to be the best aerial combination in State's history."

Whittemore glanced briefly toward Chip. "Tims Lansing is from my hometown, and he's one of my best friends, Frank. I thought *he* was State's varsity quarterback."

"Only for one reason," Dodd said quickly. "Chip was a freshman! Wait until this fall!"

"Oh, a freshman!" Whittemore said, his voice tinged with sarcasm. "Most kids can play freshman football." He looked Chip over and measured him critically again, a smile hovering on his lips. "It's quite a jump from the freshman team to the varsity. Kids don't have much of a chance. Well," he said abruptly, turning away, "see you all at the meeting tonight."

CHAPTER 2

The Six-O'clock Club

THE VIDEO was instructive as well as entertaining. It presented a complete story of the previous summer's activities at Camp All-America. It showed the arrival of the campers: some in cars with their parents, some by chartered bus from the city, and some by the shuttle bus service from the Mecklenburg Regional airport. The staff members whooped derisively when they saw each other appear on the screen, but they quieted down when the camp action began.

It seemed to Chip that the camp plunged right into its regular daily program without a single rehearsal. Assemblies, waterfront activities, fishing, boating, games of all sorts, group competitions, drama, arts and crafts, hikes and overnight trips, individual and group instruction in various skills, and finally, the season-closing celebration.

Chip sat enthralled. What an opportunity for a youngster! An opportunity to enjoy a healthy summer vacation and to develop his swimming and diving and handling of a canoe or a sailboat. It also meant a chance to participate in team games and sports supervised by expert counselors and coaches. Chip was thrilled he would be in a position to contribute to the program. Now he understood how Rock felt and what the veteran coach meant by his comment about the opportunity to work with kids—for a summer or a lifetime.

The high point of the video was a camp pageant. The staff and campers joined in the glittering ceremonies, highlighted by a water show. The climax of this event was a perfectly executed triple somersault by Philip Whittemore. It was a beautiful dive, and the commentator ended the video with the statement: "And that completes the story of Camp All-America."

Behind Chip, in the darkness, someone snickered. Then a voice whispered sarcastically, "You mean Camp Whittemore!"

Chip was surprised, but he forced himself to ignore the speaker. The comment was unfair about someone who was only doing his job and trying his best to perform a difficult feat. Personal likes or dislikes had nothing to do with it.

The lights snapped on, and Frank Dodd moved to the platform. "That's the movie we had made last summer, guys," he said proudly. "Its purpose is first as a historical record, second as a marketing promotion for new campers, and third as a visual manual to follow in preparation for this year's operation. We'll make another one this summer and add a few more details of life here at Camp All-America.

"I know that it's been a long day for some of you, but I want to run through the tape again so Cliff can make a few comments about our camp rules and safety procedures."

Chip had immediately liked Cliff Burdette. Now, as he listened to the camp director's comments, he knew the reason. Burdette took his job seriously, realizing the tremendous responsibility he and his staff faced in assuming the care and safety of nearly three hundred youngsters.

Burdette was thorough and precise, pausing the tape from time to time and reversing it frequently for playback and comments. Chip noted the great amount of emphasis he placed on precautionary measures.

"Every boy must be under supervision every minute of the day and night. Furthermore, the lakefront and pool are never to be used without supervision. Special care is absolutely necessary with respect to the use of boats and the diving tower."

There was more and it was all important, all vital to the safe operation of a boys' summer camp. Chip was more excited than he'd been in years! That enthusiasm carried back home to Valley Falls when he called his mom to tell her he had arrived safely. He was relieved to hear her voice. Yes, her recent checkup had gone very well, and yes, Hoops was his usual stubborn cat-self.

Chip's laptop had survived the trip, and he promised he'd E-mail regularly. They talked about the Hilton Athletic Club members, lifelong hometown friends, dropping by to visit before starting their summer jobs. Biggie Cohen was working at the Valley Falls Pottery. Soapy Smith was keeping his old boss, Petey Jackson, busy at the Sugar Bowl. Red Schwartz was on the grounds crew at the River Run Golf Course, and Speed Morris was dividing his summer between his dad's law office and Coach Bob Knight's Basketball Camp.

Chip went to bed that night tired but thrilled with the prospects of a happy summer. He awoke at dawn but turned over for a few more *Zs*. Then it happened. Someone banged on the door and stumbled into the room. Before Chip could face the intruder, he was grasped by the shoulder and pulled half out of bed. He sat bolt upright to face a freckle-faced youngster who was about twelve or thirteen years old, a boy he had never seen before.

"Hey!" the boy said brightly. "I'm Jimmie! Get up! Dad wants to see you! You're invited to the Six O'clock Club."

"Jimmie? Jimmie who? Six O'clock Club? What for?"

"Jimmie Dodd. You know my Dad. He owns the place! He wants to play football!"

"Play football," Chip repeated, regarding the boy suspiciously. "You wouldn't kid me, would you, Jimmie?"

"About football? Nobody, but nobody, kids about football around here."

"Jimmie, did you have too much sugar at breakfast?"

"Too early for breakfast! C'mon! Dad says you can kick a ball a hundred yards. He's kiddin', isn't he?"

Chip nodded. "If he's talking about me, he's kidding. I'll be with you in just a second, but I still think it's some kind of a joke."

Jimmie Dodd regarded Chip with solemn eyes. "I thought you knew my dad," he said seriously. "This is no joke. It's just the beginning. You see, Dad thinks he's a coach. He's been coaching Nitwhitty for years."

"Who's Nitwhitty?"

"You'll find out! Are you coming or not?"

"Chill, Jimmie," Chip replied, tying his shoes and smiling.

Jimmie led the way, and Chip followed, prepared for anything. He had heard of camp jokes and tricks and was surprised when he turned toward the row of cabins in

Olympic Village to see Frank Dodd and a boy he figured was the other son waiting on the sideline bench of the football field. Jimmie tugged at Chip's arm before they reached hearing distance. "Just humor him, and you'll be all right."

"Humor him?"

"Sure! We all do! What have you got to lose?"

Dodd smiled happily when they reached his side and then introduced his other son, "This is Frank Jr. Surprised when Jimmie woke you up?"

Chip nodded. "A little," he admitted, making certain reservations under his breath. "I was awake though. I'm usually up early at home and school."

Dodd nodded with approval, "Great! It's the best time of the day to work. So let's get started. What do you want to do? Take a few laps, kick a few, or do some passing? Guess we ought to do some stretching and a little running first. Come on!"

Jimmie and Frank seemed to know the routine. After a few minutes of pretend stretches, they fell in behind their father, and Chip followed. As they jogged around the track that circled the field, he tried to figure it out. One thing was sure—Frank Dodd Sr. was serious. *And, Chip mused, he's in shape and can run. So can the kids! Now I'm beginning to understand what Rock had in mind when he said I'd have a chance to keep in shape.*

Dodd ran easily and led them around the track at a steady pace. Frank and Jimmie dropped behind at the very start, so Chip shortened his stride and jogged along beside them. Frank was a quiet boy, just the opposite of Jimmie. After shaking hands with Chip, he hadn't said a word. But not Jimmie. He kept up a steady patter, all about football, even while they were running. Ahead of them, the camp owner kept going, looking back from time to time and windmilling his arm for them to hurry up. But the boys were unfazed and trotted patiently along without changing speed. Chip could see this was old stuff, mere routine as far as they were concerned.

The three of them were fifty yards behind the elder Dodd's second lap, and when they finished, he was waiting impatiently beside the bench and tossing a football from one hand to the other. "OK," he said briskly, "a little life now! I'll snap the ball. Chip, you do the kicking. Frank, you and Jimmie chase. On the double now, let's go!"

Chip dropped back twelve yards, and the ball came back fast, waist-high, and a bit to the right. He grunted in surprise. It was a perfect spiral. Dodd could center a ball, all right.

Chip loosened up slowly, met the ball easily, and finished smooth. He hadn't kicked a ball since the previous fall, and the kicks were traveling about forty yards. Jimmie was clearly disappointed, his disgust registering every time he threw the ball back. Frank took it in stride, booting several return kicks that equaled Chip's boots.

After ten minutes or so, Chip felt right and began meeting the ball with his long, powerful stride and an ankle snap at impact. Then the ball began taking off in high, pointed spirals, that sailed yards over Frankie's and Jimmie's heads time after time. That did it! Jimmie perked up immediately and began hustling the ball back, and Frank's face brightened with a broad, admiring smile.

Dodd was beaming. "You can really kick, can't you? I was beginning to wonder a bit, and Jimmie was ready to quit. You've got him sold now! I was kidding him, and I told him you could—"

"Could kick it a hundred," Chip said. "He told me."

"He would!" Dodd growled affectionately. "Well, that's enough of that. We'll placekick a few and then have some breakfast. Oh, and by the way, I want you to have breakfast with the family from now on. We eat early, you know, before the rest of the coaches and counselors. It gives us a chance to talk a little football."

Chip thought that over while his boots were splitting the uprights from various angles and distances. Was this going to be a daily routine?

Frankie was kneeling seven yards behind the ball, handling the passes from his father perfectly. The precision and steadiness with which he placed the ball on the ground reflected long practice. Jimmie was chasing the kicks, standing behind the goal, gleefully flinging his hands over his head every time the ball sailed between the uprights. Catching the ball, he would sprint upfield until he reached his throwing distance and then zip the ball to his father. It was fun.

Frank Dodd was enjoying it, too, even though his job was the tough one. "All right," he said reluctantly, "that's it! Hit the showers! Breakfast is in fifteen minutes. You better wear a camp warm-up suit for these workouts from now on, Chip. Bill Smith's got a dozen of them in the camp store. Come on now, Jimmie, let's have a little life."

Breakfast was a revelation. The main dining room was empty, but Chip spotted the family in a little alcove near the kitchen. Deana Dodd greeted him brightly, and after Jimmie said grace, Chip's camp initiation continued.

Mrs. Dodd started it off, "I see they didn't waste any time, Chip. I hope they didn't wear you out, or worse, scare you off. You see, I'm used to this. My husband thinks he's still playing college football. And Frankie here plays quarterback on his high school team. So far, Jimmie has concentrated on baseball. He was Little League all-state last year and won a solid gold baseball."

"Don't worry about Jimmie," Dodd interrupted. "He's going out for football this fall. Aren't you, Jimmie?"

Jimmie scowled and buried his nose deeper into his cereal bowl. The expression on his face clearly indicated he was fed up with football, especially at six o'clock in the morning.

"Chip," Deana Dodd said abruptly, "I've often wondered how a quarterback can remember all the plays. How many plays did you have to know last year?"

Chip nearly dropped the pitcher of milk. The shocked expression on his face must have given away his thoughts. *Oh, no! Not Mrs. Dodd too!*

Mrs. Dodd wasn't kidding. She repeated the question. "Maybe I didn't put the question very clearly, Chip," she said earnestly. "I'll try again. You see, I know each play has a number of variations—or what you call option plays—but there must be a certain number of basic plays. Isn't that right?"

Chip gulped and glanced warily around the table. "Er . . . yes," he stammered, "that's right. We used about sixty basic plays last year, but, of course, each one had four or five variations."

"That means you had to know about 250 plays!" Frankie exclaimed.

Chip smiled. "It's not as difficult as it sounds. You see, the basic plays are changed to meet the different line defenses the other team may be using."

"But don't opposing teams shift their defenses?" Deana Dodd asked. "I mean, don't they shift their defense after you come out of the huddle, after you've called the play?"

Chip nodded. "Yes, unfortunately, most of them do. That's why we have so many variations. In the huddle, the quarterback calls the play. Then, when the team gets up to the line of scrimmage, the other team may shift into an eight-man line or even a five-man line with three linebackers. If the original play called for blocking against a seven-man line, and the other team shifts into a five-man line when the team gets up to the line of scrimmage, the quarterback gives a code signal—an audible. This audible changes the blocking assignments to meet the five-man line and the new alignment of the linebackers."

Dodd had been moving restlessly in his chair. He was itching to get a word in somewhere and jumped right in as soon as Chip finished. "You see, Deana," he said proudly, "that's exactly the way I explained it. Tell her about the option plays, Chip."

"In high school, we used the T-formation," Chip explained. "The option plays develop after the center has snapped the ball to the quarterback. Coach Ralston uses the split T at State, and the quarterback runs a lot with the ball. I didn't play varsity, of course, but I studied all the plays. In fact, I used to practice the quarterback fakes and spins and handoffs and laterals every day in my room."

Frankie was eating up every word. He leaned forward impulsively and grasped Chip's arm. "Will you teach me all that stuff, Chip?" he asked eagerly.

"Sure," Chip said, "but it takes a lot of practice—"

"He'll practice," Dodd said grimly.

"You mean you'll both practice," Mrs. Dodd said, smiling at her husband. "Now you're in real trouble, Chip. By the way, you didn't finish the option play."

"Well," Chip continued, "when the quarterback carries the ball, he usually runs laterally right or left behind the line, and if he sees a good opening, he holds the ball and keeps going. If the hole doesn't open or if the one he's trying to hit closes up, he passes to one of the other backs or an end coming around behind the play. Of course, there are other options for the rest of the backs on certain plays."

During the football talk, there had been little eating at the Dodd table, except by Jimmie, who had already finished. Now, as various members of the staff began to drift in and "Good mornings" were exchanged, Chip, who was facing away from the main dining room, had an opportunity to concentrate on his food. Jimmie, sitting directly opposite, suddenly wrinkled up his nose and muttered, "Nitwit."

"Jimmie!" Dodd hissed. "Stop that!"

"Good morning, Whitty!" Deana Dodd called. "Sit down. We've just started."

Frank Dodd turned and smiled up at Philip Whittemore. "That's right, Whitty," he said, motioning to the vacant chair beside Jimmie. "Sit down. We've been talking—"

"Football," Whittemore added. "I might have known." He dropped down into his chair, elbowing Jimmie in the process. "Hi ya, squirt," he said, ruffling Jimmie's hair. "Did you work out this morning?"

Jimmie glanced up, dislike written all over his face, and edged his chair away as far as possible. Just as he was about to speak, Frank Dodd hurriedly cleared his throat and interrupted. "Yes, he worked out, Whitty. Where were you?"

"No one told me—"

Dodd shot a quick glance in Jimmie's direction, "You may be excused, Jimmie. I want to see you in the office right after breakfast."

"Chip's been telling us about quarterback plays, Whitty," Mrs. Dodd said nervously. "I never realized it was so complex."

"Me either," Frankie interposed. "Chip had to memorize more than two hundred plays!"

"Two hundred plays!" Whittemore echoed. "Yeah, right! No one can memorize that many plays."

"They do at State!" Dodd asserted. "At least the quarterback does."

"Well, maybe," Whittemore said doubtfully, "but it sounds bogus to me. I played two years at Central, and we only had forty plays." He rose slowly and looked questioningly at Chip. "What kind of a coach did you *have?*"

The blood mounted swiftly to Chip's cheeks. No one—but no one—could criticize Henry Rockwell. *That* he couldn't and wouldn't take. He had difficulty stilling the rush of angry words demanding utterance, but he controlled his emotions and spoke clearly and coolly. "I had the best coach in the country," he said crisply. "He had the best high school coaching record in the country for thirty-seven straight years. And he's Curly Ralston's first assistant right now—at State!"

Whittemore rose slowly from his chair, looking at Chip with feigned astonishment. Then he bowed with exaggerated politeness. "Oh," he said sarcastically, "now I understand everything! Big break for State. You and your high school coach! Hmmm. Poor Tims Lansing!"

CHAPTER 3

The Big Five

THE INCIDENT did not pass unnoticed. Almost everyone in the room noted the sharp verbal exchange and watched Whittemore stalk angrily out of the building. Bill Smith flashed a side glance toward Joel Goldstein, who answered with a slight nod. They left the dining hall together.

"He hasn't changed a bit," Goldstein said shortly.

Smith grunted his agreement, "You're right. I don't think he'll ever grow up."

"Hilton seems like a nice kid. You might know Whittemore would start on him."

"Yeah," Smith added. "Any newcomer who looks like competition gets the Whittemore treatment. But Mr. Whittemore may be in for a surprise. Hilton's stats at State were something most can only wish for. Ralston says he's a real player with a great attitude and a tremendous work ethic."

"Frank says the same thing about Whitty."

"Only one thing wrong! Frank coaches football in the summer for fun, and Ralston happens to be the head coach at State and coaches football for a living."

"Wonder what the argument was about?"

Smith pursed his lips and shook his head. "Well," he said dryly, "Whittemore's been the golden boy around here for a long time. It's my guess he didn't like a newcomer moving in, especially one who's got a solid reputation."

They strolled silently along, past the swimming pool, and down the wide walk leading to the highway. Smith broke the silence and said thoughtfully, "I wish Frank would stop this summer football madness or foolishness or whatever you want to call it."

"Oh," Goldstein drawled, "I don't see any harm in it, Bill. It's about the only fun he has, other than the kids. Goodness knows he's busy the rest of the year, giving speeches to various groups and schools, recruiting campers, keeping this place in repair, and lining up the staff."

"You're right, I suppose," Smith agreed. "I guess it isn't too serious. One thing I know for sure. He'll be heartbroken if Whittemore doesn't show up at State this fall."

"I thought he was already committed to State."

"He is, but you know Whittemore. He might decide to go elsewhere. Lots of colleges would be glad to welcome a player like Whittemore with two years of college competition under his belt."

"Do you think Frank is worried about that?"

Smith nodded. "Of course. Whittemore knows it too. He'll hold that over Frank's head all summer. Not in so many words, you understand, but the threat will be there."

"So he doesn't go to State. It isn't important, I suppose, that Frank has to put up with a lot of Whitty's nonsense all summer, is it?" Smith didn't answer and Goldstein prodded him. "Well, is it?" he demanded.

"Not necessarily, Joel. But Frank will overlook a lot if he thinks it will mean something to State's football team. Well, talking about it won't help." He glanced at his watch. "We'd better go back. We'll be late for the coaches' meeting."

After Whittemore left the table, Chip excused himself and returned to his cabin in Olympic Village. There, to keep his thoughts off the unpleasant episode, he wrote a long E-mail to his mom. That made him feel better, but he was still bothered. He stretched out on the bunk and folded his arms behind his head. Just about the time he was fully relaxed, Jimmie Dodd marched in and flopped down on a chair. Then he folded his arms and glared at Chip without saying a word.

"What's the matter with you?" Chip questioned.

"Nothing!"

"Must be something."

"Aw, Dad bawled me out for not telling Nitwhitty about the workout this morning. He said I didn't have any manners."

"Calling people names isn't good manners."

Jimmie's scowl deepened. He thrust out his lower lip and glared at Chip with unblinking eyes. "Maybe you're right," he admitted reluctantly, dropping his eyes. He sat quietly for a long minute, thinking. Then, suddenly, the sullen expression on his face vanished as if he had snatched off a mask.

"Hey!" he shouted. "I forgot! Frankie said you told Nitwhitty where to get off! Man, were we ever glad! The Nitwhitty thinks he's king around here and pushes everyone around. Frankie said you gave it to him good. I got a favor to ask. Do you think you can find time to show me that quarterback faking stuff? This afternoon?"

"I thought baseball was your game. I didn't know you were interested."

"Well, I am!"

"Since when?"

"Since this morning! I'm not giving up baseball, but I'm going to do a little concentrating on football. You know why?"

Chip shook his head. "No. Why?"

"Because Frankie gets all the breaks on account of his being on the high school team, and I get all the grunt stuff to do. I got the idea this morning. You remember what I said about humoring Dad? Well, while he was lecturing me just now, I figured I wasn't being very smart. Why get pushed around, right? Well, right then I made up my mind. I'm gonna be a better football player than Frankie and Mr. Nitwhitty too! That is, if you'll teach me. Will you?"

"I might if you stopped calling people names."

"You mean like nitwhitty, knucklehead, dork, screwball, and things like that?"

"That's right."

The scowl and glare flashed back, and Jimmie crossed his arms again. Chip met the sullen stare and waited. Suddenly, Jimmie dropped his hands to his hips and grinned. "It's a deal," he said, leaping to his feet and extending his hand. "Shake! You won't hear me call anyone 'Nitwhitty' again, ever." Then, in a sudden burst of generosity, he added, "Or dork or screwball either! Hey, if you're going to the staff meeting, you better hurry. C'mon. I'll go with you. Remember now, first lesson this afternoon."

Chip was in solid with the Dodds. In fact, he was flanked by two of them throughout the meeting: Jimmie on one side and Frankie on the other. Burdette, Smith, and Goldstein discussed their programs and introduced each of their head counselors.

Chip received a nice hand; his two companions started the clapping and continued after everyone else had stopped. Although he didn't mean to make comparisons, Chip couldn't help but notice that Whittemore received only scattered applause. He joined in, but Jimmie and Frankie literally sat on their hands. Chip thought he saw Jimmie's lips forming a familiar expression, but no sound escaped, so he put it off to his imagination.

After the meeting, Jimmie again reminded Chip of his promise. "Three o'clock, Chip. I'll bring the ball. Frankie wanted me to ask you if he could come too. It won't hurt if he just watches, will it?" Chip assured Jimmie he didn't mind if Frankie watched. Chip laughed and added, "I'll be glad to work with both of you."

Jimmie backed away from that suggestion. "No way, Chip. This is a deal just between you and me. Remember? You help him in the morning. That's enough!"

Although it was Saturday and camp did not officially open until Monday, many campers arrived early and were soon scattered all over the place. Most of them came down to the football field to watch the practice, and some of the bolder ones joined right in, much to Jimmie's annoyance. But he was a good sport about it and kept Chip busy shaking hands with counselors and campers. Sunday was the big day. So many youngsters kept coming that Chip thought there must be a thousand of them instead of almost three hundred. Before he had time to wonder where the days had gone, it was Monday morning, and Jimmie was pulling him out of bed.

"C'mon, c'mon, Chip. It's six o'clock! Dad and Frankie are already out on the field. And, Chip, Nitwh—" Jimmie swallowed hard and continued meekly,"Uh, Whittemore's out there too."

"That's all right, Jimmie. The more the merrier! There are no hard feelings between Whittemore and me as far as I'm concerned. Let's go."

Chip wasn't too sure about that, but he hoped it was true. He didn't want to be at odds with anyone. Since the episode at the Dodd breakfast table, he had seen Whittemore only a few times, and then at a distance.

Before he turned the corner of the last Olympic Village cabin, Chip heard the commotion, but he was unprepared for the sight. The football field was swarming with football players and hopeful football players. Chip recognized most of them as counselors. They were darting downfield for passes, shouting for the ball, whooping it up, and having a great time.

Dodd, seeing Chip and Jimmie, motioned vigorously. "Come on, you're late. Stretch and then two laps for you guys."

Jimmie started out and Chip followed. Jimmie was really putting out. "C'mon, you," he shouted, "turn it on, turn it on!"

When they finished their laps, Dodd blasted the whistle around his neck. "All right," he shouted, "let's have a little organization here! On the double now, everyone over there by the bench."

Chip was amazed. The wannabe players were as enthusiastic and full of energy as if they were members of a regular football squad and Dodd was their coach. When they grouped at the bench, Dodd gestured for quiet.

"We're taking up right where we left off last summer. I'm sure glad to see so many of you the first morning. Right now, I want to say I was more than proud of each of you who made your team. As for those who didn't make it, well, you'll make it this year!" He paused and looked at Jimmie before continuing. "Why, I'm even counting on Jimmie making his middle school team." He winked at his listeners. "I think he'd trade his gold baseball for a football right now."

The remark drew a laugh as Dodd had intended, but Chip noticed that Jimmie squared his jaw and clenched his fists. "You're in for a surprise, Mr. Dodd," Chip murmured to himself. "A big surprise. Frankie isn't going to be the only football player in your family."

Dodd poured it on that morning. First, it was passing and receiving with Whittemore and a tall, lanky counselor doing the throwing. Chip took his turn with the rest of them. He enjoyed the thrill of plucking a high pass out of the air while running at full speed. But he never had a chance whenever he was on the receiving end of one of Whittemore's tosses. The ball flew far over his head when he was downfield and into the dirt on the short bullet passes.

Midway into the practice some important spectators appeared: Burdette, Goldstein, and Smith. They sat down on the bench and watched the young athletes. These men were athletes too—perhaps not physically capable of competing with the players working on the field, but they were far ahead of them when it came to experience and know-how. They knew and appreciated good football. Smith and Goldstein exchanged knowing glances when Whittemore winged a long pass far over Chip's head, but it was Burdette who voiced the criticism.

"Whitty must be trying to show how far he can throw it," the camp director observed dryly.

"You mean show up Hilton," Smith corrected.

"The kid can move," Goldstein remarked. "Really move!"

"He can pass too," Smith added. "I saw him put on an aerial show at State last Thanksgiving that I'll never forget. If that big show-off," he nodded toward Whittemore, "ever wises up, the two of them will be unstoppable."

"He'll never wise up," Burdette said in resignation. "Looks as if they're through. Let's go."

Chip hurried through his shower and was one of the first to show up at the dining hall. Instead of going inside, he sat down on the top step and tried to figure out how best to approach Bill Smith with his situation. He was still trying to frame the words when the sports director walked up the steps and sat down beside him.

"Some workout, Chip," Smith said lightly. "Develop a good appetite?"

"Sure did," Chip said quickly. All sorts of ideas were racing through his mind. This was the opportunity he had been hoping for, but how should he start? Then he plunged in. "Mr. Smith, do you suppose you could work it so I can have breakfast at the staff table as well as lunch and dinner?"

The corners of Smith's mouth lifted, and his eyes twinkled. "Oh, I guess so," he said lightly. "Any special reason?"

"No, sir. That is, I think I can do a better job if I don't get any special favors."

Smith nodded understandingly, "You're absolutely right. Tell you what, we'll sit here and catch Frank as he comes in to breakfast."

"I just wouldn't want Mr. Dodd to think—"

"Skip it," Smith said briskly. "He'll understand."

While they waited, Smith talked about Camp All-America, outlining the purpose and aims that made it a different camp, a camp where every boy was a special project. "It was Frank's idea, Chip," he explained. "I guess Frank was thinking about the kind of camp he'd like his boys to attend. At any rate, his thinking resulted in the philosophy that guides us now."

Smith paused a moment and then continued slowly, choosing his words carefully. "No two boys are alike, Chip. Every youngster has a hidden spark and requires a lot of observation and study before anyone can really understand what makes him tick. Most people judge a youngster by his personality. But lots of boys—and girls, too, for that matter—have a reserved personality and take some time to get to know. The old saying 'You can't judge a book by its cover' just about expresses the point.

"Anyway, we, and I'm speaking for all of us—Frank, Burdette, Goldstein, Scott, and myself"—he grinned— "we're called the Big Five—well, we chart every camper and keep a folder to collect all sorts of information about his attitude, physical characteristics, and levels of skill improvement. This information is gathered from the counselors, head counselors, coaches, and instructors."

"What about his friends, the guys who bunk with him?" Chip asked.

Smith nodded. "Good question. Every week, the five of us," he hesitated and chuckled, "the Big Five, get together and discuss each boy and plot his progress. Then one of us has a little personal chat with those who need help. For example, one of the boys assigned to me may be overly shy and need someone to draw him out. It's my job during the next week to see that the camper makes progress in that particular area. The following week, someone else gives him a whirl. Frank usually sums up our observations and progress charts and then talks to the camper personally. That's where the real job is done, and I don't know anyone who could do a better job. Frank has something that inspires a kid's confidence."

THE BIG FIVE

"It must take a lot of time."

"That's why we're here, Chip. We're not running this camp to make money. Most of our profits go toward giving worthy kids who don't have money an opportunity to attend our camp. As far as time is concerned, there are lots of kids here who never need help, usually kids we've had two and three years."

"I guess you turn out some pretty good athletes."

"Sure do! Most of the kids we classify as seniors are top athletes and regulars in some sport in prep or high school. And I don't believe there's a college in this part of the country where one of our former campers isn't an outstanding athlete.

"But don't get the idea we go overboard on team sports. Actually, we're more concerned with individual sports and the development of the kid's character and personal confidence than we are in team games. Our country needs kids with strong bodies as well as good minds, Chip. You see—Hold it, here's Frank."

Frank Dodd was cooperative, but he didn't like it. "Bill, Frankie and Jimmie are counting on learning a lot of football from Chip. Why, Jimmie's almost forgotten all about baseball. And with Chip and Whitty both at the table, those two kids—"

"They'll learn a lot more out on the field, Frank," Smith broke in softly. "And Chip and I can do a lot more for *three hundred* kids."

There was no answer to that! Chip breathed a deep sigh of relief. Now he could concentrate on his job.

CHAPTER 4

The Silent Treatment

CHIP CONCENTRATED on his job, all right. Bill Smith made sure of that by setting a pace any athlete would have found difficult to match. Chip's duties kept him busy every second. Starting each morning with the six o'clock football workout, he hustled until camp curfew, supervising the activity program of forty of the youngest campers and their five counselors.

Curfew didn't end the day. Chip still had the responsibility of checking his section and making sure everything was shipshape for lights out. Chip was in charge of five cabins in Olympic Village; each housed eight boys and a counselor. It was his job to coordinate the progress of each of his groups from one instructor to the next and from one activity area to another without conflicting with the progress of the other three sections. Philip Whittemore, Ray Belding, and Ben Solomon had similar assignments.

Chip was Bill Smith's assistant, and his special assignments focused on team sports. Whittemore assisted

THE SILENT TREATMENT

Blaine Scott with social activities and drama, while Ray Belding worked with Cliff Burdette, helping with individual sports. Ben Solomon was Joel Goldstein's waterfront assistant. The Big Five, coaches, head counselors, counselors, and counselors-in-training all assisted in special camp events.

The program was fast and absorbing, and the days sped by so rapidly that the camp had been in operation a week before Chip had time to sit down and think things over. As much as he enjoyed his work, something out of place was bothering him. Jimmie hadn't called him in the morning, and neither of the Dodd boys had shown up for the early football workout. Whenever Chip glanced at the Dodd table in the dining room, Philip Whittemore seemed to be talking with enthusiasm, but only Frank Dodd seemed interested. Jimmie and Frankie kept their eyes focused on their plates, never looked up, and never once ate a bite. Neither of the boys seemed to be around during the day. Curiosity finally got the best of Chip, and he queried Bill Smith.

"What in the world is wrong with Jimmie and Frankie Dodd?"

"Oh, that! I thought you knew. They're giving Frank the treatment."

"The treatment?"

"That's what they call it. They're on a lockjaw strike."

"Lockjaw strike?"

"Yes. Won't talk, won't eat, won't work!"

"Sounds silly. What's it all about?"

"Well, knowing Jimmie and Frankie and knowing their dislike for some of the members of the staff—without mentioning any names, of course—I imagine it has a lot to do with football before breakfast, during meals, and all day and all night in winter, spring, and summer."

Smith glanced at Chip. "Now don't get yourself all upset. Those kids know their way around Frank Dodd, and they'll come out on top. Get set for a surprise."

Chip got the surprise that evening. When he entered the dining room, there were two new guests at Bill Smith's table. Jimmie and Frankie sat there grinning like two Cheshire cats.

"Hi ya, Chip! Hi ya, Coach Smith! Have a seat. Make yourselves at home. Like to join us?"

Smith grunted knowingly. "We will. Well, what have we done to deserve this? How come?"

"Perseverance," Jimmie muttered. "Pigheaded perseverance plus mulish disrespect for our parents."

"Dad's exact words," Frankie explained glibly.

"You two don't look underfed to me," Smith observed dryly. "Probably spent all your summer's earnings in the snack bar."

Jimmie nodded vigorously. "You're right," he admitted. "Now, Chip," he said briskly, "we can get back on schedule. See you at six in the morning."

Back on schedule, Jimmie and Frankie showed up at six o'clock the next morning to pull Chip out of bed. After workout and breakfast, he found the twosome waiting in the athletic office.

"Dad said we were to work with you," Jimmie explained.

"That's right," Frankie said gleefully. "He's washed his hands of us and said he'd fire all three of us, you too, if he saw Jimmie or me anyplace but with you every day for the rest of the summer."

"You're hooked, Chip," Jimmie said, grinning impishly, "for the whole summer."

The boys proved to be good workers. They knew the camp and its routine. With their help, Chip's program was soon running like a clock. Chip got plenty of help from his counselors. He had gone all out in his endeavors to win their respect and cooperation, and now it was paying off. He was able to devote more time to the paperwork Smith kept piling on his desk.

The athletic office was located in the Dr. Naismith Field House. Chip's desk was beside a picture window overlooking the waterfront of Bailey Lake. The office walls were covered with charts, schedules, and programs; there was a sports calendar literally for every hour and every day of the eight-week camp session.

A few mornings later, Chip was working at his desk while his two new "assistants," Jimmie and Frankie, were sitting at a nearby table laboriously printing a bulletin-board notice. The campers from Chip's section were reviewing their individual basketball videotapes and watching highlights of the NCAA Final Four with their counselors.

Down on the lakefront, some distance away, Joel Goldstein and Ben Solomon were teaching some campers how to swim. Chip watched them, impressed by their patience with the little guys.

Out on the diving raft, Philip Whittemore was supervising his section's lifesaving techniques. Chip shifted his attention to watch this important camp feature. Three of the counselors were working with their charges in the waist-high water beside the pier that jutted out into the lake. Out near the diving raft, another counselor and three of the smaller campers were slowly paddling away from the diving raft in a canoe.

Chip couldn't figure out what it was about the scene that alarmed him. But he had a feeling of fear, a presentiment of danger, that something wasn't right. Perhaps it was because the three boys in the canoe were so young—too young, in his opinion, to tip over a canoe and swim fifty feet or more to the raft. "I don't like it," he muttered, rising and casting a quick glance at Jimmie and Frankie. He hurried out of the office and down toward the lakefront without disturbing his two friends.

Chip slowed his pace, forcing himself to walk slowly toward the water. *What's the matter with me?* he asked himself, casting a quick look at Goldstein and Solomon, who were near the pier and farther up the shore. *This is a regular lifesaving drill, and Whittemore's an expert. It looks like every one of these kids can swim like a fish.* But he was still unsettled. He couldn't go along with the idea of one counselor, expert or not, assuming the responsibility of safeguarding three boys in a canoe. "Two would be bad enough," he murmured. Continuing his leisurely pace, he watched the counselor and the boys tip over the canoe. The young swimmers struck out for the float while the counselor remained beside the floating canoe.

Suddenly, one of the boys began to thrash the water. "Help!" he cried out. "Help!"

The frightened boy's companions turned around immediately and began swimming toward him. Chip hesitated a second and then dashed out along the pier, discarding his sweatshirt as he ran. The stricken boy's friends had now reached his side, and Chip could hear Whittemore shouting orders to the counselor, who was swimming to the rescue.

Just as Chip reached the end of the pier, he was horrified to see the desperate camper struggling fiercely with his would-be rescuers. All three were now in serious danger. The next moment, Chip was in the water and swimming with every ounce of his strength toward the scene.

As Chip drew nearer, he saw the drowning boy had locked his legs around one of his friends and was trying to climb on top of the other. Then the boy tumbled back, and all three went down together. Only one came up; he was gasping for breath and barely able to keep his head above water. Chip and the counselor dove at the same time, but it was Chip who found the locked bodies and grabbed, fought, and pushed them to the surface.

The counselor bobbed up beside him, and they pulled the boys apart and started for the shore. Chip looked for the other boy and saw him a few feet away, treading water and trying to regain his strength. Then he saw Whittemore clinging to the canoe.

"Help him, Whittemore!" Chip shouted. "He can't make it!"

Whittemore pointed down toward his leg and shook his head. "I can't!" he cried. "I've got a cramp!"

Chip held the half-drowned, frightened little boy and looked desperately around. The counselor had his hands full with the other boy, and Chip wasn't sure he could handle both boys. But he had to try.

"Hold on, Chip!" someone shouted. "Just a second now."

Goldstein and Solomon arrived in a lifeboat and hauled the boys aboard. Goldstein went right to work on one boy while Solomon took care of the other.

"Help Mark into the boat, Chip," Goldstein said briskly, motioning toward the counselor. "He can row us ashore."

Chip boosted Mark into the boat and turned back to the canoe, noting Whittemore's pale face and trembling lips. "Hold tight," he said. "I'll tow you in."

Whittemore seemed to be in great pain; he was grasping the canoe with one hand and rubbing his leg with the other. But when Chip's feet touched bottom and he turned to help Whittemore, the big diver brushed him off and hurried past without a word. Chip followed and was relieved to see all the boys were all right.

Goldstein glanced up, smiling grimly. "Nice work, Chip," he said gratefully. "You too Mark. It might have been serious if you two hadn't been on your toes." He turned back to the boys. "All right, you young swimmers, Mark will take you to the infirmary so Dr. Bayer can look you over. You'll be fine in a couple of hours and back swimming before you know it."

Chip retrieved his sweatshirt and started to remove his wet, soggy socks. Up ahead, he could see Philip Whittemore striding along with his section, railing at his counselors with every step. "Whittemore got over his leg cramp pretty fast," Chip mused. "Come to think of it, he wasn't limping when he waded out of the water. How come?"

Jimmie and Frankie came running up then and thumped him on the back and pumped his hand.

"You were great, Chip!"

"We didn't know you could swim like that!"

"We saw the whole thing from the office window!"

"Boy, wait until I tell Pop!"

"You got it! C'mon, Frankie, we gotta get going!"

"Where are you two going?" Chip questioned suspiciously.

"Around," Frankie said mysteriously. "See you at lunch."

Jimmie and Frankie made the rounds, and by lunchtime everybody in camp knew Chip Hilton had proved himself a hero that morning. Jimmie was good at multiplication, and by the time he headed for the dining room, Chip had, according to Jimmie, saved nine campers, three counselors, and one visiting parent.

All this publicity resulted in a standing ovation for

Chip when he entered the dining room at noon. The campers cheered and stamped their feet, and Frank Dodd gave official sanction to the tribute by congratulating Chip in front of the assembled group.

"Chip, I guess the applause speaks for itself. Everyone here is proud of you. We've never had a disaster at Camp All-America, but this morning's experience was too close for comfort. Thanks to you and Mark King our record still stands.

"You know, there's an old saying that it's an ill wind that blows no good. So there will be some new regulations in effect as of this afternoon covering swimming and lifesaving tests. I might add that the three campers in this morning's waterfront drama are in fine shape and will be out of the infirmary this afternoon."

Chip didn't like it. It was all nonsense. Why embarrass a person for doing what anyone would have done?

Frankie tapped his brother on the arm. "Hey, look at Whitty. Look at that face!"

"Right!" Jimmie exclaimed delightedly. "Man, he looks like he's been raised on lemons." He nudged Chip. "Look at him, Chip. Look at that face!"

Chip wasn't a bit interested in Whittemore's appearance, but he glanced toward the Dodd table to please Jimmie. The boy was right. The big athlete's face was flushed with anger, a complete reversal from the pale, uncertain expression he had worn while clinging to the canoe. That quick glance was enough. Chip wanted to eat his lunch and get out of there as quickly as possible.

Bill Smith understood how Chip felt and steered the conversation away from the morning's event. And that took strategy, because Jimmie and Frankie were interested only in their new friend's sudden rise to fame and only wanted to talk about Chip's morning adventure. It embarrassed Chip, and he was glad when the meal was finished and could ask to be excused.

But Chip couldn't escape entirely. During his rounds that afternoon he had to face the fact that all the campers in his section were sold on Bill Smith's assistant, Chip Hilton. It was the first time they had shown any real affection for him, and he didn't exactly know how to act. But it made him feel good and strengthened his resolve to do a good job.

Chip loved his work, and he especially enjoyed the opportunity to observe the coaching staff's methods and techniques. These men were experienced teachers, and many of them had been famous athletes. Coach Dong Shul "Don" Kim, A & M's famous Olympic track and field coach, was Chip's favorite instructor. Kim was a fine organizer and a firm believer of group work in teaching. He used the counselors to assist him in teaching the campers sprint starts, baton passing, proper takeoff for the long and high jump, footwork for the shot put and discus throws, and other track fundamentals. The kids moved from one assignment to the next as if they had been going through these drills for months instead of only ten days.

Chip was learning more at this camp than he had dreamed possible. Smith was teaching him how to plan and organize a program and coordinate one group with another. And he was learning a lot about teaching and coaching from the high school and college coaches who supervised the various sports. He was so absorbed in watching Coach Kim work with the boys that he didn't know Bill Smith was standing beside him until the camp athletic director cleared his throat.

"Pretty good, isn't he?"

THE SILENT TREATMENT

"He's great, Mr. Smith. He must have been studying track all his life."

"There's more to it than study, Chip. Some things can't be learned from a book. You have to love your work and you have to love kids. Don Kim wouldn't trade jobs with the president of the United States. He loves kids. That's why he's such a good teacher."

CHAPTER 5

"Anything You Can Do . . ."

FOOTBALL HAS an unbelievable fascination for some people. It gets into their blood when they are young and courses through their veins as long as they live, sometimes exerting an influence on everything they do.

Frank Dodd had never forgotten his football days at State. Next to his family and Camp All-America, football was the dominant factor in his life. Dodd's enthusiasm for the game was a terrific motivator for the members of his Six O'clock Football Club, and they gave the workouts all they had. Chip would have preferred to skip the practices, but the intense determination of Jimmie and Frankie to master the T-quarterback play was a challenge. Besides, he liked Frank Dodd.

The counselors quickly realized that Chip Hilton and Philip Whittemore were the two best football players in camp. Whittemore was the bigger of the two and tried to do everything in a big way. When he was punting or placekicking, he tried to boot the ball out of sight. Chip, on the other hand, concentrated on timing, tough angles, and good placements.

When Whittemore was passing, he overthrew most of the time, seeming to find a peculiar pleasure in firing the ball far beyond the receivers. Chip's passes were right on target—fluffy, fingertip tosses anyone could pluck out of the air. The counselors liked Chip's passing and let him know it.

"Couldn't miss it if I tried, Chip!"

"I had to catch it or get hit in the nose!"

"That's threading the needle, Chip!"

Frank Dodd was in heaven. Here, right at Camp All-America, he had one of the greatest passing combinations in the history of the collegiate game, and he announced the fact to everybody in sight.

This particular morning, Bill Smith and Blaine Scott showed up to watch the early workout. During the first break, Dodd ambled over to the sideline. "Ever see anything like those two?" he asked. "Ever see any better kicking and passing? Watch this!"

Whittemore was sprinting down the field, chasing a long pass that Chip had winged far ahead. Just when it seemed hopeless, he leaped high in the air and pulled in the perfect toss.

Dodd turned back to Smith and Scott. "Well," he demanded, "what about it?"

"Most anyone looks good in practice," Smith said dryly.

"But you yourself said Hilton was the greatest passer you ever saw."

"I still say it."

"I don't understand—"

Scott interrupted. "I'm not a football expert, Frank, but maybe this will explain it. You remember that old song that says 'Anything you can do, I can do better; I can do anything better than you,' or something like that?"

"Sure! What's the connection?"

"Nothing much, except that Whitty seems to feel it applies to Chip Hilton."

Dodd shook his head. "That's stretching it a little too far. Whitty hasn't got a jealous bone in his body, if that's what you mean. He just puts out all the way in everything he does. You've got him wrong."

"*I* haven't got him wrong, Frank," Scott said slowly. "I know Whitty very, very well. He's worried about Hilton's popularity, and he's been trying to show him up, to the neglect of his job. He spends more time showing off on the trampoline and the diving tower than he does with his section, and I don't like it."

"Have you spoken to him about it?"

"Yes, I have."

"What did he say?"

Scott shrugged his shoulders. "He said you gave him permission to practice anytime he wanted and that his counselors were old hands and knew what to do." He grinned wryly and continued, "Whittemore had the nerve to say he'd spoken to you about keeping an eye on the new head counselors—meaning Hilton, naturally, since he's the only new one—and said that was the reason he hadn't been with his own section as much."

Smith grunted. "Wish he'd done a little more than keep an eye on Hilton down at the lake the other morning," he said pointedly.

"He had a cramp in his leg, Bill," Dodd said defensively. "Even then he had enough courage to stick to the job and tell Hilton and King what to do."

"That's his story," Smith said shortly. "What's this business about keeping an eye on Hilton?"

"Perhaps that's my fault, Bill," Dodd explained. "We were talking about Hilton at dinner one evening, and I said it would be nice for him to give Chip a hand, to help break him in so to speak."

"He'll break him, all right," Smith said bitterly. "I suppose I ought to start practicing on the trampoline and the diving tower now that Whittemore's taken over my job."

"Now, Bill," Dodd said softly, "don't get upset. Whitty just misunderstood, that's all. I'll straighten him out. See you at breakfast."

Smith and Scott watched the practice for a short time and then walked slowly away. Smith was seething. "Imagine," he said sarcastically, "imagine the nerve of the guy. He'd keep an eye on the new staff."

"He twists Frank around his finger."

"He twists other things too. I'd better talk to Hilton before there's a real run-in. I don't think Chip's the type to take much shoving around."

Chip was eager to get through practice and breakfast. This was a big day in his camp life because it marked his first personal contribution to his section's program. He had planned a boxing tournament, and Coach Smith had given his approval. For the past week, Chip and his counselors had been teaching the youngsters and classifying them according to age, height, weight, and coordination. The big day had arrived, and Section E campers of Olympic Village were assembled in a roped-off area of the field house. The gloves were massive twelve-ounce pillows, but they were fine for Chip's purpose.

Each cabin from Section E was represented by several contestants, two seconds, and a counselor as an adviser. Chip served as referee. The campers cheered their favorites enthusiastically and ribbed their opponents unmercifully. But the boxers were serious and went toward one another with more enthusiasm than effectiveness during the one-minute rounds. Just as the third bout ended, Philip Whittemore came pushing through the crowd to the side of the ring and bellowed belligerently at Chip.

"What's going on here? Who gave you permission to stage this special event?"

Chip was surprised. "Coach Smith, of course," he said uncertainly. "Is there something wrong?"

"Of course," Whittemore growled. "It's a good thing I checked up on you. All exhibitions are under the supervision of my department! Break it up now and get back on your regular program." He turned his back on Chip and motioned to the boys surrounding the ring, "Now beat it! All of you!"

Chip's counselors had their campers stay where they were and began muttering rebelliously.

"Wait a minute, wait a minute there!" Chip called. "Don't be so fast. This is just a boxing tournament in my own section."

"It's an exhibition," Whittemore roared, "and I'm ordering you to end it right now! Right now, you understand? Right now!"

Chip smiled grimly and shook his head. "Sorry, Whittemore, I'm not cutting it out. This section is under my supervision, and I take orders from Coach Bill Smith. I suggest you consult him before trying to tell me how to do my job." He climbed back up in the ring. "Come on, guys. Who's next?"

"I'll see Smith, all right!" Whittemore shouted angrily. "And Frank Dodd too. Remember, I warned you. If one of these campers gets hurt, it'll be your responsibility."

"ANYTHING YOU CAN DO . . ."

Jimmie Dodd just couldn't resist and shot back, "This isn't the waterfront, ya know."

Whittemore ignored Jimmie and looked Chip up and down contemptuously. "If you were a little bigger, I'd give you a real lesson with the gloves!" he snarled. "Teach you a little sense."

"Yeah, right! On the same day you teach lifesaving skills again!" Jimmie shouted.

It was hard to take, but Chip ignored Whittemore and called for the next bout. This break had been coming for a long time. Perhaps it was just as well that it was now out in the open.

Whittemore hurried out of the field house and headed straight for Frank Dodd's office. He had a feeling he had come off second best in the argument, but that wasn't too important. Frank would take care of Hilton, he told himself. He barged into Dodd's office without knocking and flopped down in a chair beside the desk.

"You look upset, Whitty," Dodd said solicitously. "What's the matter?"

"Two words! Chip Hilton!"

"What about him?"

"He's staging a gang fight down in the field house. And when I tried to break it up, he as much as told me to go jump in the lake."

"A gang fight?"

"That's right! Some of those kids are going to get hurt."

Dodd picked up the phone. "I'll call Bill and tell him."

"Hello, Bill! Frank! Say, you know anything about a gang fight that Hilton's section is mixed up in? . . . No? Well, Whitty says there's some trouble brewing. You'd better check it out. Someone might get hurt!"

TEN SECONDS TO PLAY!

Dodd slapped his desk sharply and faced Whittemore. "Bill will take care of it, Whitty. You just run along now and forget the whole thing. Thanks for reporting so promptly. Oh, by the way, Whitty, if Hilton's so touchy, perhaps it would be better to let him work out his own troubles. OK?"

Whittemore nodded and stomped out of the office. Hilton was going to run into some trouble, all right, he vowed. He'd see to that personally.

Bill Smith doubted there was much to check. But he hurried down to the field house and stopped inside the door to survey the crowd. "What was Whitty talking about?" he asked himself. "This is no gang fight. This is great!"

Unnoticed, he stood at the back of the group and laughed at the roundhouse swings. What the boxers lacked in science, they made up for in exuberance.

When the bout ended, a great cheer broke from the campers. This was action. "Can we do this again? We want more of this!" one camper yelled. "Now *this* is a real camp! Let's go, E, let's go!"

Bill Smith waited for Chip at the door. "Nice idea, Chip," he commented. "The kids love that sort of stuff."

"I thought they liked it, but I was a little worried."

"Worried? What about?"

"Well, Phil Whittemore said something about it being an exhibition, and I thought—"

"I know what you thought, Chip," Smith said understandingly. "Forget it."

On their way out of the field house, the two passed several groups from other sections, and the campers all yelled, "Hey, Chip! Hey Coach Smith!" and waved.

"That I like," Smith said proudly. "Come into the office. I want to talk to you." He preceded Chip and went directly to his desk. "I want to make a call, Chip. I'll only be a second."

He picked up the phone and a moment later was speaking to Frank Dodd. "Hello, Frank. This is Bill. I just checked that item. Nothing to it. . . . What's that? . . . No, nothing of the sort. I can't talk now. See you later."

Smith's blue eyes were twinkling when he turned back to Chip, "Now, let's you and me have a talk.

"We've got a wonderful bunch of kids here, Chip, and you've made a fine start as a member of the staff. Curly Ralston and Henry Rockwell gave you fine commendations, but we prefer to judge an employee by his performance on the job. Let me ask you something. Have the kids in your section played any tricks on you? I mean, harmless jokes?"

"No, sir. Not yet."

"Well, they will now."

"Why now?"

"Because you've proved yourself, Chip. The kids know you now, and they'll stick with you forever. There's just one little mistake you might make, one way you could lose their trust.

"You might soften up because of their admiration and let them get away with something that may seem harmless enough but goes against the rules. You see, Chip, we're aware of the little harmless tricks boys play on those they respect and love, and we always overlook them, even though we may pretend to be terribly upset.

"But once in a while, a boy who isn't sure of his position with the other boys or one who wants to be a leader and doesn't know how tries to be different. He tries to show his independence and gain leadership by breaking the rules. Most of our kids are at an impressionable age and admire courage, guts if you will. But the wrong kind

of kid capitalizes on this type of admiration and sometimes leads other decent kids into trouble. You have to be
on the watch for this kind of boy all the time, Chip, and
if you find him, you have to step on him promptly and
mercilessly. I guess you've heard the old adage about the
one bad apple in the barrel. Well, that applies to members of the staff as well as to campers. You see, Chip, taking care of boys, taking care of the hearts and souls of the
parents, so to speak, is a responsibility that can afford no
mistakes and no omissions in the line of duty, no matter
how trivial they may seem.

"I didn't mean to lecture, Chip. I just wanted to com-
pliment you on a fine start. And, Chip, the only bosses
you have here are Frank and Deana Dodd, Cliff
Burdette, Joel Goldstein, Blaine Scott, and myself. I
guess you understand what I'm trying to say. Anyway,
keep up the good work."

If the jokes played on him reflected his popularity,
Chip Hilton was the pride and joy of Section E. First, it
was his bed. He found the sheets folded halfway up, his
pajamas soaked in water and knotted tight, the pillow
full of rocks, mud in his toothpaste tube, and a number
of bullfrogs and garter snakes for roommates. It was all
in fun, and Chip joined in the laughs at his expense.
Then he pulled a few on the campers, sending them on
fool's errands for left-handed monkey wrenches, sky
hooks, striped paint, and the key to the pitcher's box. The
whole camp was soon buzzing about the good times in
Section E.

Chip was especially wary on the lights-out check,
and for good reason. The first warning came when he
found the night light completely out in Cabin 5. He knew
something was up but pretended to be annoyed by the
missing light. Groping around in the dark, stumbling

over shoes, overturned chairs, duffel bags and soap, he located what felt like the light cord. He grasped the cord to steady himself, and then it happened. Up above, on the rafter, there was a jangle and a swish, and then a tub of water overturned and came swooshing down, soaking him from head to foot.

"Wow!" Chip howled, gasping for breath. "Who did that?"

Instantly, coincidentally of course, someone found the real light cord, and as the lights flashed on, Chip found himself surrounded by all the campers of Section E. They were under beds, on the floor, on trunks, everywhere, whooping and laughing at his drenched appearance.

"Joke's on me," Chip gasped, wiping the water from his face. "Wow! How in the world did you get all that water up there?"

The payoff occurred the next morning. Jimmie and Frankie tugged and pulled him out of bed, laughing more with each passing moment. "Hurry, Chip, hurry!" Jimmie shouted. "Everything's up in the air!"

"Yeah, Chip," Frankie added. "Check out the flag-pole!"

Chip followed them outside, and there, strung on a line running all the way to the top of the flagpole, was every item of Chip's wardrobe: shirts, pants, swimming trunks, T-shirts, shorts, socks, shoes, and sweaters. Every sleepy-eyed member of Section E was shouting with glee.

"Oh, no!" Chip gasped. "What next?"

Wearing his only nonflying shorts, Chip pulled down the line and began removing his possessions. The removal of each item raised another cheer and lots of advice. The commotion attracted campers of other sections, and a roll call would have found a few campers missing. From that time on, Chip never lacked for advice concerning his attire. In fact, the campers discovered certain items Chip never remembered owning.

That night when Chip made the lights-out check, it was raining. He entered each cabin with special care, but nothing happened, and he went to bed worn out and ready for a good night's rest. The patter of the rain on the cabin roof and the rustling of the pine trees made him drowsy. But, as usual, when he was dead tired, sleep came slowly, and, what sleep he got was disturbed by dreams. Perhaps *nightmares* is a better word.

Just when he was about to tumble off the flagpole in one of the nightmare episodes, Chip was startled out of his sleep by a crack that shook the cabin, rattled the chairs, and nearly tumbled him right out on the floor. Chip's first thought was of firecrackers. It was another trick.

"Now, what?" he managed. "What can they be up to this time?"

CHAPTER 6

Thunder and Lightning

CHIP STRUGGLED to his feet, half awake. The cabin trembled and shook under thundering blasts, and every piece of furniture in the room seemed to dance. Flashes of lightning pierced the inky darkness and reflected on the windows. These flashes continued, accompanied by claps of thunder, torrents of rain, and a whistling wind that grew in intensity. As he stumbled across the room to the light switch, he could hear the straining and snapping of branches and the banging of flying objects outside the cabin. He snapped the switch, but the power was out.

"It's a bad storm," he told himself. "I've got to hurry!" He quickly pulled on jeans, sneakers, and a camp T-shirt and fumbled for a flashlight. Through the windows he could see that the entire camp was pitch dark, the blackness broken only by brilliant flashes of lightning. He pushed on the screen door cautiously and succeeded in opening it about a foot. Suddenly, the door was torn out of his hands and right off the hinges. It banged against the side of the cabin and took off with a clatter toward the swimming pool. Directly ahead, on the tennis courts, a streak of lightning hit a light pole and exploded with a tremendous blast, illuminating the entire camp for an instant.

Chip dashed for his next cabin, soaked to the skin before he had gone ten feet. Streaks of lightning were darting everywhere, in front of and behind him and all around the cabins ahead. The wind was like a tidal wave, buffeting him in every direction. He fought his way to the first cabin and dragged his wind-tossed body through the door. "Get away from those windows!" he shouted. "Lie down on the floor! Here, here in the center of the cabin. Now stay there! Keep them right there, George, until I get back!"

He hurried into each cabin, repeating his instructions. The lightning seemed to be concentrating in the area of the cabins now, and Chip dashed for the end cabin, muttering a prayer that he would be in time. Banging against the door, he forced it open and found everyone safe.

"We're all right, Chip!" Fred Stone called from the group of campers lying on the floor in the center of the cabin. "We're fine. But you better check Whittemore's section. His groups are running all over the place!"

"Nice work, Fred!" Chip shouted. "Wonderful! Be right back. Keep 'em right where they are."

He dashed outside to face flashes of lightning playing round the buildings. Then he saw what Fred meant. Ahead, in Whittemore's section, he could see campers dashing wildly from cabin to cabin.

"Get in those cabins!" he shouted, forcing his way forward. "Inside! All of you!"

Rushing the youngsters, he herded them inside the first cabin. "Who's in charge here?" he shouted. "Get them down! No moving around and no standing up. Andy, you're the counselor. Take charge!"

Again he dashed from cabin to cabin, bolstering the courage of the counselors and assembling the campers. "One more," he breathed. "Only one more."

Then he was running toward the last cabin. He caught a glimpse of the wide-eyed faces of young campers pressed against the panes of the windows.

"Oh, no!" he shouted. "Get down, get down!"

Inside, the cabin was chaos. The boys were congregated at every window, scared half to death. "Get down!" he yelled, trying to top the frenzied sounds of the storm. "Get down! Come here! Sit here in the center of the cabin!"

There was a blinding flash and a sharp explosion just outside the cabin door, and then every object and every face jumped out at Chip as clear as a picture on a screen. The bolt of lightning hit the ground between the tree line and the last cabin. The cabin rocked! The screen door was thrown off its hinges, and the wooden door flew back into the corner of the cabin. All the windows on that side were shattered!

It was over before Chip could move, and then he heard someone shriek in pain and saw three campers lying on the floor. He sprang into action and with the help of the other campers carried them to the bunks nearest the center of the room. "His leg's cut, be careful!" he cried. "Cover the other two with blankets."

Chip was worried. The darkness and bolt of lightning had been too much for these kids, and they were approaching hysteria. "Come on," he said sharply. "We've got work to do. Someone get the first-aid kit. It's on the shelf in the bathroom. Who's in charge of this cabin?"

No one answered, and Chip repeated the question. Again there was no answer. Perhaps they hadn't heard him, Chip mused. They were probably scared out of their wits. "All right," he asked calmly, "can any of you guys talk?"

Still there was no answer, but one of the boys handed him the first-aid kit. Chip found the smelling salts and soon brought the two semiconscious boys around. They complained of headaches and felt sick. Chip looked at the cut leg of the third boy. It didn't look very deep. He stopped the bleeding and put a gauze wrap over the area.

"It's a cut, all right," the youngster said bravely, "but it doesn't hurt much."

Fortunately, there was an interruption. Bill Smith and Joel Goldstein came rushing in, carrying large flashlights. The kids crowded around, everyone talking at once, each giving his own version of the incident. As soon as the storm had subsided, Smith and Goldstein escorted the three boys to the infirmary.

Chip remained in the cabin with the kids, and a few minutes later the lights flickered and came on to stay. Cheers sounded from all over the camp, and Chip's companions calmed down.

"Chip, we were scared stiff. We didn't know what to do."

"Boy, were we lucky. You think Dan and Herb and Buddy will be all right?"

Chip assured them that they would be fine and then repeated his earlier question. "Who's in charge here?"

Again there was silence and averting of eyes. Chip gave up. They heard him, all right. They had heard him all along. It wasn't too important. He could find out easily enough. Where could the counselor have gone? And why hadn't Whittemore shown up to take care of his section?

Daylight brought a shock to everyone at Camp All-America and to hundreds of motorists driving along the highway. The camp had been right in the path of the severe summer thunderstorm, and the beautiful grounds were strewn with shutters, chairs, small trees, and debris of every kind. Plants and trees were uprooted along the highway, numerous windows had been broken, and several roofs had been lifted cleanly from nearby houses. But there had been no other camp injuries, and the three boys from Section D were all right but resting in the infirmary for observation.

Jimmie and Frankie had been all over the place, inspecting everything, and when they found Chip they reported in detail. Frankie started it off. "Jimmie caught it from Pop," he announced abruptly. "He ran out of the house in his pj's, right in the middle of the storm, to go to the office to get his gold baseball. Pop chased him and gave him a good walloping. I didn't know Pop could run so fast. Boy, was he mad!"

Jimmie nodded impishly. "Yep, that's right. Pop should've gone out for track. He can move for an old guy. Oh, have you seen the cabin that was hit? You can see the hole in the ground right beside the cabin where the lightning hit."

"You hear about Whitty?" Frankie demanded, continuing before Chip could answer. "Lightning got him! Right in his own cabin, right inside the door. Knocked him out cold. He's all right though. Hey, time for food! C'mon, Jimmie. See you later, Chip."

Chip strolled slowly toward his campers' cabins, giving himself a good lecture on the way. He was completely disgusted. *What's the matter with me anyway? I didn't even give Whittemore a chance, just because we had a run-in. It wasn't any of my business! He could have been caught in an emergency the way I was. And all the time I was wondering about him, he could have been killed. I'm too suspicious.*

TEN SECONDS TO PLAY!

As Chip approached his cabins, a young man detached himself from a group of campers and approached. Chip recognized him as a member of Whittemore's staff and sensed that he was the missing counselor.

"My name's Dan Pryor, Chip. I work with Whittemore. I'd like to talk to you about last night, but I don't know what to say. The kids told me about the great job you did, and I want to thank you from the bottom of my heart. I know you're wondering what happened to me. I'd give anything if I had been here, but you see Whitty said he'd look the other way if I went to this party at another camp. He also said that he'd look in on my cabin and do the headcount for me. I told my kids where I'd be."

Pryor looked hopefully at Chip and waited. But Chip couldn't answer right then. In fact, all the time Pryor had been talking, Chip had heard another voice—Bill Smith's voice—as clearly as that day in the office. "You see, Chip, taking care of boys, taking care of the hearts and souls of the parents, so to speak, is a responsibility that can afford no mistakes and no omissions in the line of duty, no matter how trivial they may seem."

Pryor was pleading again, striking straight at Chip's heart with every word. "You've got to help me, Chip. You're the only one who can get me out of this. I know they're going to ask you what happened and where I was. They'll fire me for sure when they find out.

"I don't know what I'll do if I lose this job. I need the money to help pay my tuition at A & M. I never spent a more miserable night in my life. When the storm broke, I tried to get a lift back, but no one would take me. Please help me out, Chip. I'll never forget it. Honest!"

There was no doubt about Pryor's sincerity. "I'll help all I can, Dan," Chip said softly, "but I won't lie if they ask me." His face brightened. "Maybe they won't ask me anything about it." Impulsively, without reservation, he grasped Pryor's hand. "I hope for your sake everything comes out all right, Dan, but we've got to face one fact: you knew the rules. We can't get around that no matter what we say."

Pryor nodded in agreement, "You're right, Chip. This is my second year here, and I know all the rules by heart. I was wrong, and that's all there is to it."

"Perhaps it would be best to go directly to Coach Burdette and tell him the whole story. I think that's what I'd do if I were in your place."

Pryor nodded thoughtfully and turned slowly away, speaking softly over his shoulder. "That's what I ought to do, I guess. Thanks, Chip."

The inquiry wasn't long in coming. A few minutes later Chip saw Dodd, Burdette, Smith, Goldstein, Scott, and Whittemore walking toward Section D with Dr. Bayer. Pryor was on the spot.

Not long afterward, Chip got all the news through the camp grapevine. Jimmie rushed in, abrupt and to the point as always. "Burdette canned Pryor, Chip. He's leaving right away. Man, was Burdette ever mad. I like Pryor. I wish he hadn't been so dumb."

Later, Chip got his information firsthand from Dan Pryor. Dan was hurt, but he was taking it the right way, and his words made it clear he felt better. "I'm leaving, Chip. I told them the whole story before they had a chance to ask. It's all over now, and I guess no real harm was done since the kids are all right.

"Chip, I told my kids the truth too. I didn't want them to think you had anything to do with my leaving. They're wonderful. I'm sure going to miss them—" Pryor choked up then and dropped his head to hide his emotion.

Chip didn't know what to say, but he tried his best. "Everything's all right, Dan. Your conscience is clear now, and you can forget the whole thing. I wish you'd E-mail me and let me know how you get along with your college plans. State plays A & M all the time, and maybe we can get together."

Pryor smiled gratefully. "I sure will. I wish—" He paused again and then continued in a rush of words that showed how much he was hurt. "I wish Whitty was like you. Burdette asked him about it, and Whitty said he thought I was kidding." He smiled bitterly. *"Kidding!* I don't understand it. Then Whitty said I was a veteran and knew the rules. That's right, of course, but I thought he'd at least tell Burdette he had promised to cover my cabin. Thanks for what you did to help, Chip. I'll never forget it."

"I didn't do anything, Dan."

"You did more than you'll ever know. And, Chip, I'll send you an E-mail. See ya."

Then Pryor was gone. Chip sat alone, thinking how easy it was to make a mistake, how trivial things seemed to grow and grow until they were real trouble. Coach Burdette probably would have given Pryor the evening off if Dan had told him that Whittemore was going to supervise his cabin. Chip tried to force the thought out of his mind, but it kept coming back. Whittemore had to be in the wrong in some measure. That is, if what Pryor said was true. And there seemed to be no point in Dan lying about that part of the trouble.

Chip was startled out of his thoughts by Jimmie's return. The grapevine was at it again. Chip wanted no part of the camp gossip, but he had about as much chance of shutting up Jimmie as he had of turning off Niagara Falls. Jimmie's face was serious, and, contrary to his usual explosive delivery, his words came slowly and thoughtfully.

"Chip, you think lightning can go in a house and hit someone and go right out without leaving some sort of a sign or a mark or something?"

Chip shook his head uncertainly. "I don't know enough about lightning to answer that, Jimmie. Why? What's on your mind?"

"Well, you know the holes the lightning made in the ground next to the cabin and how the door was smashed and the windows broke? Well, I checked Whitty's cabin, and there isn't any damage anywhere. Not outside, not at the door or the windows or the walls or anyplace else."

"I don't see what that's got to do with it, Jimmie. Maybe he was outside when he got hit."

"No! Whitty said it came right through the door."

"Maybe the door was open. Lightning does some tricky things."

Jimmie pursed his lips and eyed Chip speculatively. "I guess," he agreed. "You're right. But it isn't only lightning. Some people I know around here do some tricky things too."

CHAPTER 7

The Bear Facts

JIMMIE DODD liked a person or he didn't. There was no middle ground with Jimmie in anything. He left abruptly, completely disgusted with Chip's lack of insight, put his head down, and charged into his father's office. "Dad, I want to talk to you!" he demanded.

Dodd arched his eyebrows. *"That's* different," he said dryly. "What do you want to talk about?"

"Dan Pryor. He got a bad deal!"

Dodd raised his hand in protest. "Now, Jimmie—"

Jimmie imitated his father perfectly, raising his hand in protest and saying, "I know, I know. That's not for me to decide. I'm *too* young to make serious decisions. I've had no experience, and I don't know the facts. But this time—" He paused and glowered at his father belligerently. "This time I have the facts!"

Dodd sighed. "Proceed," he said submissively.

"Well, I talked to Dan's campers this morning, and they told me they were right there when Whitty said he'd take care of them while Dan was at the party at that other camp."

"That doesn't excuse Pryor, Jimmie. Cliff was the proper person to ask. Perhaps the boys misunderstood what they were talking about."

"They didn't misunderstand," Jimmie said stubbornly.

"Now, Jimmie, Whitty's been with us for years and—"

"Sure! But did he ever do anything around here except brag about his football and swim and dive and have a good time? And did he ever save anybody, or ever do anything in an emergency?"

"Stop!" Dodd said sharply. "That's irrelev—"

"I know," Jimmie said resignedly. "It's irrelevant, immaterial, inconceivable, inconsequential, insignificant, incompatible, and . . . Oh, forget it!" He turned and left.

Frank Dodd got a big kick out of his sons, enjoyed their moods, and was thankful his work gave him the opportunity to share their lives. He had them figured out pretty accurately too. Jimmie wasn't the type to go to bat for anyone unless the person deserved it. "An eye for an eye and a tooth for a tooth" was Jimmie's philosophy. Dodd couldn't understand why Jimmie had formed such a violent dislike for Whittemore. It wasn't like his son.

The revelation that Whittemore knew Dan Pryor was going to be out of camp without permission was a surprise, but Dodd felt he knew Whittemore so well there must be a satisfactory explanation. He decided to check on that right away and paged Whittemore.

A few minutes later the big athlete strode into the office and dropped down in a chair beside Dodd's desk.

"You want me for something, Frank?"

"Yes, Whitty, I do. I'm a little worried about Pryor. I understand he claims you knew he was going to the party and had promised to cover for him. Is that so?"

"It certainly is not. I thought he was joking, especially when he asked me in front of all the kids. I told that to Burdette right in front of Pryor." Whittemore spread his hands in a gesture of futility. "I couldn't help it if he just up and took off, Frank."

Dodd nodded. "I know, Whitty," he said with understanding. "Forget it."

That afternoon Chip received a letter from Henry Rockwell and a football video he had requested from State's football office.

> *Dear Chip,*
>
> *Received your letter last week. Hope you're enjoying that easy camp life. Everyone here is fine and I am enjoying a good rest and getting ready for training camp. I suppose you received your notice to report to Camp Sundown. Actually, you'd better do some running. It won't be long now.*
>
> *One of the football secretaries told me she mailed the football video yesterday. I'll make sure you receive a film each week.*
>
> *Coach Ralston sends his regards and suggests you get acquainted with a veteran counselor there at camp by the name of Philip Whittemore. He played junior college football last year and was rated among the outstanding small-college receivers in the country.*
>
> *Coach Ralston says Whittemore is already enrolled here at State, and I*

*know Curly's counting on him to bolster
our weakness on the receiving crew.
Perhaps the two of you can find time to
work out some passing patterns.*

*I saw your mom last week, and she
told me you were enjoying your work. She
looks fine. Don't worry, I'll keep an eye on
her health for you.*

*Saw the Hilton Athletic Club crew at
Trullo's Bakery the other day. Soapy and
Biggie said to say hi—they're having a
good rest too! Speed's back from basketball camp and is now in his dad's law
office. He says his dad and Coach Knight
are a lot alike. Red's got a great tan from
working on the golf course. Can't play any
better, but he says he's great on the mower.*

*As ever,
Coach*

That night the entire camp watched State's football
video. State's T-quarterback wizardry made such a hit
that half the camp turned out the next afternoon for
Jimmie's special football workout. Everybody wanted to
learn to be a quarterback like John Elway. At least, it
seemed that way to Chip.

Jimmie had read somewhere that an aspiring quarterback should carry a football around with him all the
time. Naturally, he came dashing up with a ball under his
arm and took charge. "Let's show 'em how it's done, Chip,"
he said importantly. "Now move back, you guys. We'll
demonstrate the whole works. I'll center the ball. C'mon,
Frankie, you, Bill, and Skip be the backs. Let's go!"

Chip executed the pivots, feints, handoffs, and passes in slow motion and then at playing speed. The older campers seemed to take in every movement Chip made. The younger ones couldn't follow the ball, but they ate it up, applauding time after time. Then Chip really went to work, showing the campers how to conceal the ball behind a crooked elbow, behind the back, and under crossed arms. He asked if they had any questions.

"College quarterbacks have to know all that stuff?" one youngster asked.

Chip grinned, "T-quarterbacks have to know it."

"You must have practiced a lot," another boy volunteered.

"I guess so. I practice every chance I get and almost every night before the mirror in my room."

"This faking stuff. Is it important? I mean, does it really fool the other team like it fooled us?"

Frankie answered that one. "Important? Fool the other team? Good grief, Chip even fools his own teammates. Sometimes he gives me the ball, and I don't even know I have it."

Chip didn't know Whittemore was watching until the big athlete laughed derisively. "Listen to the mutual admiration society," he said mockingly. "You guys plan on *talking* football or *playing* football? If you're going to play, you'd better start working. Season's almost here."

"What's with you?" Frankie demanded belligerently.

"Softly," Jimmie growled. "Whitty got hit by lightning. Remember?"

Chip ignored the remarks. "He's right," he said quickly. "State's fall training camp opens in three weeks."

"Three weeks!" Jimmie exclaimed. "We *do* have to get to work. I've got football stuff to learn before camp closes."

"You can say that again," Chip agreed. "Hold it a minute. I want to show Whittemore a letter from my coach."

Whittemore was a bit surprised, but he took the letter. As he read, an amused smile formed on his face. "He overlooks a couple of things," he said, tapping the letter with his finger as he returned it. "First, I'm registered at State, all right, but that doesn't mean I'm going to show up."

Whittemore paused to let that sink in and then continued. "Another thing you might or might not like to know is that Tims Lansing and I are buddies. That's one of the reasons I'm considering State. Tims and I have been practicing pass patterns for years." He paused and grinned arrogantly. "So I can't see much advantage in working out with you, Hilton. Tims has been State's regular quarterback for the past two years, and I don't think any freshman flash is going to beat him out, even if he does have some hokey high school volleyball coach pulling for him. See you around."

Chip took a step forward, hunching his shoulders and balling his fist, before he remembered himself. Whittemore was trying to bait him. He relaxed then and watched Whittemore swagger away. Whittemore had tried to really diss him. Chip shrugged and turned back to the kids. At least, he'd done his part and tried to cooperate. From now on, he'd stick strictly to his own business. As far as Tims Lansing was concerned, well, time and Coach Curly Ralston would have something to say about State's starting quarterback.

Summer was coming to a close, and the weeks flew by almost as fast as days. Camp activities kept pace, with new events crowding one another for completion.

TEN SECONDS TO PLAY!

One of the big events was the Bear Mountain outing, and everyone in camp was excited when the day arrived. Everybody in camp went on the trip, leaving Camp All-America at 5:00 A.M. for a full day of fun and sport.

Buses transported the cheering, singing, happy campers to the famous resort. The outdoor breakfast with each camper doing some chores—gathering wood, cleaning grills, building fires, cooking bacon on hot rocks, toasting bread on sticks, covering spuds with mud and roasting them in the embers, taking turns cooking flapjacks, and generally getting in the cooks' way—was a glorious event.

The same wild confusion reigned at lunch. Every minute of the day was filled with activity: supervised swimming in the pool and lake, boating, tennis, fishing, horseback riding, hiking up to the main buildings, competing in special games and contests, and finally, assembling for the big event of the day—the mountain climb.

It wasn't much of a challenge as far as mountain climbing was concerned, but everyone pretended it was the real thing. Section E of Olympic Village led off, following a trail thousands of vacationers walked during the summer. Near the top, Chip called a halt. Most of the campers dove into their trail snacks, while others explored the mountainside.

Suddenly, a cry of alarm rang out, followed by the sounds of running feet and panting campers. Seconds later, two of the younger boys came tearing out of the underbrush. "Bears!" they shouted breathlessly. "Hundreds of them! All over the place! One of them nearly tore us to shreds!"

Section E assembled as if by magic, every member wide-eyed with fear, surrounding Chip as if drawn by a magnet. Chip was apprehensive until he saw the boys were wholly unharmed. Then he realized instantly what had happened and couldn't resist a grin. "I don't see any scars," he observed. "Are you sure the bears were after *you two?*"

The startled boys nodded vigorously. "They sure were! They were all around us! I don't know how we got away!" They looked nervously over their shoulders. "We better get out of here! They're probably on the prowl or something!"

"Probably," Chip agreed dryly. "By the way, how did you two get over that steel fence?"

"Fence? Yeah, that's right. There was a fence." The taller boy looked abashed and sighed deeply. "Man," he said, "they sure gave us a scare!"

"That's understandable," Chip said lightly, mentally kicking himself for his oversight in failing to take the boys to see the bears. He turned to the boys surrounding him and motioned for them to sit down. "Now, listen. There are bears here in Bear Mountain Park. That's where the park got its name. But they're all fenced in and they're harmless. This is a state park, and you can be sure the authorities wouldn't let bears roam around free. Of course, one might break loose."

"Wow!" one boy observed. "If any of those grizzlers get loose, I'm heading home!"

"They're not *grizzlers*," Chip corrected. "But if one got loose, it would be wise to leave him alone."

"What if we're all eating, and a gang of them charges us and wants to sit in?" another little camper asked.

"Well," Chip said, chuckling, "I've heard two ways of protecting yourself. The first way would be for each of us to climb a tree and let them enjoy themselves with our dinner. 'Course bears are good climbers too. The other way is to lie perfectly still and play dead until the bear goes away. So if any of them appear, half of you try the tree, and the other half play dead; then we'll see which works best."

Laughing, they gathered around for a campfire snack. But Chip noticed a few of the city boys looked furtively around for a nearby tree—just in case. During the meal, Chip told them about the wildlife that abounded in the vicinity and dwelt at length on the subject of deer. He explained, too, how the game laws protected them to such an extent that they were almost a nuisance.

"What a place to hunt!" someone observed.

"It wouldn't be fair," Chip said slowly. "You see, they're practically tame."

"My father got a deer once. He smashed it with his car. Yuck! He wanted to have the head put on the wall, but Mom said she'd move if he did," one young boy announced.

"I'll bet it was at night," Chip commented. "Sometimes they're frozen by headlights, and then they're just as likely to run directly toward the car as away from it. In fact, hunting regulations recognize the effect that light has on a deer, and jacklighting is against the law."

"How does this jack-o'-lantern work, Chip? When you're out hunting, I mean."

"I never saw anyone use a jacklight," Chip explained with a smile, "but when a beam of light is flashed or focused in the eyes of a deer—or most any animal at night—there is a bright reflection. The animals are often so confused they stand as if hypnotized, and a hunter can hardly miss. It's something like shooting sitting ducks, and just about as sporting too."

"Any sitting ducks or raccoons around here?" one new camper asked.

"Let's look for them! We could trap one if we had time," another camper volunteered.

"They're tough and can really fight. They drown their prey that right, Chip?"

"That's not true," Jimmie Dodd interrupted. "A raccoon is a clean animal, and he always washes his food before putting it into his mouth."

Chip didn't want to let Jimmie down, but he had no alternative. "Almost, Jimmie," he said softly. "Nature didn't give the raccoon saliva glands, so he has to wet his food in order to swallow it. Actually, he is no more finicky about his food than any other animal."

"That's a new one on me," Jimmie said thoughtfully. "Wait till the next time my mom tells me I ought to be as clean as a raccoon."

Someone brought up the subject of skunks then, and that brought a chorus of good-natured protests: "Oh, no! No skunks!"

"You're liable to meet one of those fellows anytime and just about anyplace," Chip warned. "And you'd better give him the right of way. If you meet one, just give him a wide berth. The skunk is a fine fellow if you leave him alone but a pretty tough little guy, in *his* way, if you don't. One thing is sure. He'll give you something to remember him by if you cross him.

"Here's a little saying, kind of a funny poem, but it might remind you to stay away from them."

> *There once was a boy from the city,*
> *Who saw what he thought was a kitty,*
> *He stooped down to pat the nice little cat,*
> *And they buried his clothes out of pity.*

CHAPTER 8

In a Tight Spot

CHIP'S WILDLIFE lecture was interrupted by the arrival of Olympic Village's Section D at the bottom of the sloping, twenty-foot cliff just below Section E's position. Jimmie Dodd and several of his friends sauntered over to the top of the cliff and launched some extremely pointed advice on the art of ascending a mountain. Some of Jimmie's suggestions were so startling that Chip decided he better see what was going on. Despite Jimmie's advice, however, several of Whittemore's campers mastered the assault and came panting up over the top.

Jimmie suddenly clamped Chip's arm. "Look, Chip," he said anxiously. "Look at the third one there on the ledge. I think he's sick."

The camper wasn't sick, but he sure was scared. Chip noticed the frenzied grip the boy had on a small rock and his shaking knees. He was peering down the ten-foot drop as if it were a hundred, seemingly hypnotized by the distance between himself and the rest of the group below him.

"Just a minute," Chip called, keeping his voice level and free from excitement. "Grab this rope." He fastened his rope around the base of a small sapling and let it down beside the terrified boy. It dangled in front of the boy's face, but he was too frightened to seize it. Then Chip saw Whittemore standing at the foot of the cliff.

"You better shinny up the rope and help him, Whittemore!" Chip called. "He needs you."

Whittemore mumbled something and looked up, shaking his head. Chip was startled to see that his face was deathly white, his forehead and cheeks covered with nervous sweat.

"I can't make it!" Whittemore called. "I sprained my wrist down below." He held up his right arm, showing the tape around his wrist, and added, "I haven't got any strength in it. It won't hold my weight."

Chip hesitated a second, holding Whittemore's gaze, before he slid swiftly down the rope and gained a footing beside the trembling boy. "Don't worry," he said, grasping the youngster firmly by the arm. "Lots of people get sick when they get up off the ground. Look, I'll help, but it's up to you to show you're not afraid. Come on now. We're going on up. Are you ready?"

The little camper was scared, but he was game. "All right," he managed to say. "I'll try."

Chip nodded and smiled. "I knew you had what it takes. Now you grab hold of my belt and I'll pull. Hold tight now and use your feet. There's nothing to it. Keep walking and keep looking up. Just look up and follow me. See, it's easy. All my crew went up over this rock, and you're going to do it too. Atta boy! Nice going! Now that wasn't so bad, was it?"

They exchanged a high-five, and the youngster flashed Chip a quick, warm smile of thanks as he joined the other members of his group.

"You just got dizzy," Chip assured the little guy. "You'll be all right now. That's the last tough one, and it really isn't very bad. Right, guys?"

"Sure. It was a cinch!"

Thirty minutes later, Dodd, Smith, Burdette, Goldstein, Scott, and the others who had ascended by the winding path joined the campers at the top of the mountain. The view was breathtaking, but few of the campers realized the real importance of the scenery spread out below. Frank Dodd took care of that, silencing them and explaining the part these mountains and the famous river below had played in the founding of the country. Dodd's voice was filled with pride and feeling as he talked, and the boys listened intently to his fervent description.

"While you're getting a breather, boys, I want to take advantage of our surroundings to talk about our country. Right here, we are in the midst of many historical points that remind us that this wonderful country of ours was not come by lightly. Below us is the Hudson River.

"In colonial days, there were no roads as we think of roads, only horse and oxen trails. The river was a vital water highway. Our colonial army was small, weak, and untrained. The British troops had marched down from Canada, had fought the Battle of Saratoga, and were headed for New York. General George Washington was our commander in chief, and it was most important that he learn of the approach of the British."

Dodd paused and pointed across the river. "See that high mountain? That's Mount Beacon, where Washington kept lookouts. The mountain got its name from the beacon fires his observers built as a means of signaling. Today, we use satellite communication to transmit military information. But in those days, there were no satellites, no phones, no TV, no cars, no sport utility vehicles, and no roads on which to ride like we have," he reminded them. Then he joked, "Wonder how they survived without fast-food spots?"

Dodd gestured toward the river and continued. "We, all of us, owe all our wonderful privileges to those heroes who gave their lives for freedom. The freedom you and I and our parents and friends enjoy today. Some of us have fought for our country. All of us are willing. Let us pray that we shall never again have to defend our country against an aggressor. But if we must, let us be proud to follow in the footsteps of the men and women who died for our freedom.

"Do you remember reading about Benedict Arnold in your history books? Well, right there in West Point, today the home of the United States Military Academy, such men as Robert E. Lee, Ulysses S. Grant, John J. Pershing, Dwight D. Eisenhower, Douglas MacArthur, two generals most of you will recognize—Norman Schwarzkopf and Colin Powell—and many other famous Americans were trained.

"In colonial days, West Point was a fort commanding the northern approach of the Hudson River. Benedict Arnold commanded the fort. He betrayed his trust and planned to surrender West Point to the British. Luckily, the plot was discovered in time; Arnold fled to the British troops for safety. Later, he went to England, where he died in disgrace, a fitting end for a traitor. Below us is the west anchorage of the huge hand-wrought iron chain that the colonists placed across the river to prevent ships from passing the Point."

A deep silence followed Dodd's words. It was a long, thoughtful silence, a fitting silence unbroken by a single word or movement.

TEN SECONDS TO PLAY!

Dodd himself broke the silence, arousing each youngster from his reverie. "Well, boys," he said, "you know how much emphasis I place upon athletics. But more important, much more important, is love of country. That's why I have told you these things. So now that you are rested, it's time we started for home."

On the way down the mountain, Chip couldn't stop thinking about Philip Whittemore. This was the third time Whittemore had come up with a lame excuse in a tight spot. Maybe it wasn't fair to count the storm, but the lake episode and the incident on the cliff were enough. Whittemore hadn't even made a move to try.

Whittemore failed to show up for football practice the next morning. But later in the afternoon, Chip saw him working on the trampoline, surrounded by a group of admiring campers. Chip paused to watch. After several jumps to gain power, Whittemore flew upward as though propelled by a spring, spinning like a tossed coin. He landed lightly on his feet and bounced forward in a swan dive. Just when it seemed he was going to crash to the ground, he twisted in the air and grasped the side, upright with both hands, and breaking his fall, slid lightly to the ground.

Chip walked on, amazed by Whittemore's coordination and skill. Then something struck home. Whittemore's wrist wasn't taped, and Chip had seen no sign of an injury when he grasped the trampoline upright. "I wish I could get him out of my mind," Chip breathed. "I can't figure him at all. How can he be afraid, if that's what it is, and still dive like that and play football?"

After the headcount and lights out that night, Chip hit his bunk completely tired out. "Man," he sighed, "I'll be glad when the next week is over."

Bill Smith must have realized Chip was feeling tired, because the next morning he told him to take the day off.

"We're going into town and staying all day. We both need a change of scenery. Whittemore, Solomon, and Belding are going along."

Solomon and Belding spoke when they climbed into Smith's van, but Whittemore said nothing and sat moodily silent all the way into town. Smith parked the van in the nearest lot. "We'll meet here at five o'clock. Now explore the town and forget about Camp All-America for a few hours."

Solomon and Belding started out in one direction and Whittemore in another. Chip took the first street and walked. He watched some kids in a playground, spent an hour window-shopping, and after a light lunch, took in a movie.

It was 4:30 P.M. when Chip left the theater and started back to the parking lot. He took his time, studying the people on the street and looking in the store windows. In a few minutes he was out of the main shopping section, and the pedestrians had thinned out. The street was now lined with a few bars, gas stations, and run-down houses.

Up the street, a hundred feet or so, Chip saw several men lounging in front of a poolroom. Suddenly, they erupted into action and surrounded a passerby. As Chip drew nearer, he saw that two bulky men had forced a third man up against the corner of an alley. He was just about to cross the street to avoid the argument when he realized their victim was Philip Whittemore. He hurried forward then, his heart pumping and a strange feeling of fear gripping his chest.

By the time Chip reached the corner, the men had forced Whittemore through the alley and into a vacant lot behind the poolroom. A high fence effectively blocked escape except by the alley. Several onlookers followed, and Chip trailed behind, straining his ears to learn the cause of the argument.

The men who were badgering Whittemore were tough looking. The older and rougher of the two was nearly as tall as Whittemore but much heavier. The other was shorter, big-boned, muscular, and missing a few teeth. Both were unshaven and had all the earmarks of cheap street thugs.

"So you're a wise guy," the bigger man snarled, giving Whittemore a rough shove. "Get over there by that fence, pretty boy. Now you apologize for running into me. Go on, apologize!"

Whittemore's face was pale, and his eyes darted from left to right like those of a cornered animal. "I didn't see you, mister," he stammered through trembling lips. "Honest, it was unintentional."

Chip pressed forward, his heart thumping loudly. Whittemore was in a tight spot.

The shorter man pressed forward then and shouldered Whittemore viciously. "You smart summer college guys think you own the town, don't you? We'll show you!" Carried away by his own belligerence, the man slapped Whittemore across the mouth. "You heard him!" he snarled. "Apologize!"

Whittemore was completely cowed. He fell back from the blow and retreated as far along the fence as he could go. He was trembling and trying to protect his face with his elbow.

Chip couldn't take it any longer. He pushed his way through the onlookers just as Whittemore's frightened eyes singled him out.

"Help, Hilton!" Whittemore shouted. "Help me!"

CHAPTER 9

Two on Two, Minus One

"HOLD IT," Chip said appeasingly. "What's the trouble?"

Both men whirled around, surprised by the interruption. There was a second of silence then, broken by the big man, who measured Chip speculatively and stepped toward him. "Hold what?" he demanded obstinately.

"I don't know what happened," Chip said levelly, "but I'm sure it can be straightened out without a fight."

"Oh, you think so," the smaller man said, moving away from Whittemore and giving him a chance to edge toward the alley.

"What business is it of yours?"

"None, I guess. But I know Whittemore, and I don't want him to get into trouble."

"Oh, you know him," the big man mocked, wiping his mouth with the back of his hand and moving closer to Chip. "Now isn't that sweet. You know him, and you don't want him to get into trouble. You hear that, Sam?"

The smaller man nodded. "Yeah, I heard it," he said, advancing until he was almost by Chip's side. "I heard it," he repeated, "but I don't like it."

Whittemore had taken advantage of the opportunity to get back through the alley and moved quietly toward the street.

"He apologized," Chip said calmly. "That should clear it up. Come on, Whittemore—"

But Whittemore had slipped down the alley and was out of sight. Chip turned to follow, but he didn't get far. The man named Sam grabbed him by the arm and whirled him back against the building. "Now don't be in a hurry, bright eyes. We want to talk to you."

"Yeah," the big man said softly, "we want you to do a little explaining."

Chip knew any move he made would probably precipitate a fight, but he had no choice. He pushed his hands hard against the wall and leaped between the two men and out into the open, with his back to the fence. He was still cornered, but at least he had a little room.

"I don't have a problem with you guys," he said coolly. "I don't even know you. This is silly. Now let me out of here."

"Oh, sure," the big man sneered. "We'll let you out. Get him, Sam! Let's show him what we do to college boys."

Chip avoided that first rush, realizing then he was in for a dirty street fight with no holds barred. He'd have to keep his feet. If these thugs got him down . . .

He circled, changed direction, and cut in and out, dodging the big fellow's haymakers and concentrating on the smaller man. This one was winded and knew nothing about boxing. Chip jabbed him at will, skipping away when cornered to duck inside the big man's wild swings and drive solid punches to his stomach.

TWO ON TWO, MINUS ONE

Then the smaller man took off in a running leap for Chip's knees. Chip hesitated a split second, unwilling to believe he was fighting for keeps. Then Chip met the headlong dive with the knee of his right leg, smack into the man's evil face. There was a sharp crack, and the bully rolled along the ground, groaning and holding his jaw.

"It's broken," Chip said, addressing the big man. "I couldn't help it."

He was reaching down to help his stunned assailant when one of the big man's flailing swings caught him right in the back of the neck. For a moment he thought his neck was broken. "Rabbit punch," he groaned, twisting away, barely avoiding another wild swing. Backtracking as fast as he could, he staggered with a bang against the fence. Now he was in for it.

Twisting, ducking, rolling with the punches, and gasping for air, Chip fought to keep his senses. Then the big man caught him flush in the eye, knocking his head sideways and plunging him partly through the fence. Completely at the mercy of the bully now, Chip looked up just in time to dodge the full force of a vicious kick aimed at his head. But he couldn't avoid it completely, and the shoe crashed through his protecting arm and landed on his nose, sending blood streaming over his face. "This is it," Chip muttered, shielding his face with his arms and struggling to get back on his feet.

He never knew who came to his assistance, but someone in the crowd pulled the man away just long enough for Chip to lurch to his feet. Standing there, weaving uncertainly, he was engulfed with an implacable revulsion for his vicious opponent.

"This isn't over yet!" he hissed. "I can play that way too!"

A look of amazement spread over the man's brutal face, and he grinned viciously, "OK, college boy. You asked for it! Now I'm going to knock your head clear off!"

He moved in rapidly, following Chip's weaving figure, holding his blows until he was close enough to deliver the knockout punch. That gave Chip a breather and enabled him to resume his weaving, crouching, and jabbing attack. His blows lacked steam at first, but they kept the man off balance. In less than a minute, the ruffian's face was puffed and discolored.

The big thug pulled back to clear his head. That gave Chip his chance. He hooked his left to the bully's jaw and followed with a straight right that smacked full into the man's mouth. The man tumbled slowly back, all the fight knocked out of him. In the background Chip heard someone yell, "Beat it! Cops!" but he didn't stop. He continued to rain blows until the man crumpled to the ground, out cold.

Someone took him by the arm then and handed him a handkerchief. "You've got guts, young man. No one around here ever handled either one of those two 'fine' citizens, much less the two of them at the same time."

"Thanks," Chip breathed thankfully, suddenly realizing the speaker was a police officer. "I had to defend myself. They gave me no choice."

"I know," the policeman said kindly. "Just the same, I have to have you ride with me to the station. You all right? Good! Bill, call another car to drop these two off at the hospital. Sorry, kid, it's not serious, just routine."

Smith and his three passengers had been waiting for Chip close to half an hour when the police car pulled into the parking lot and stopped beside the van. "Are you Bill Smith?" the driver asked.

TWO ON TWO, MINUS ONE

Smith smiled. "That's right, officer. Hope you're not looking for me."

"Well, yes and no. We've got a young man down at the station who's been in a little trouble. He says you know him. Name is Hilton."

Smith's eyes popped. "What happened to him?"

"Got mixed up in a little fight. You can follow us down."

Smith followed the police car in the van, talking to his passengers on the way. "I can't imagine Chip in a fight," he ventured. "Wonder what happened?"

"Beats me," Solomon said, shaking his head. "I've never seen him angry."

"Me either," Belding agreed.

Whittemore remained silent. Smith pulled into the police parking lot and hopped out. "Come on," he said. "Let's see what this is all about."

Solomon and Belding jumped out eagerly and were right on Smith's heels, but Whittemore hung back and stopped in the hall outside the open door. He remained there all through the conversation, listening intently.

Chip had cleaned up, but there isn't much that can be done for a black eye, a cut mouth, and a smashed nose, to say nothing of a face covered with scratches and bruises. Smith took one unbelieving look and whistled softly under his breath, "What happened to you?"

The police sergeant answered, grinning and chuckling, "You ought to see the other two!"

"Other two?" Smith echoed in disbelief. "You mean there were two of them?"

"That's right. We've got one of them locked up, minus most of his teeth, and the other one's in the hospital with a broken jaw. A couple of tough hombres, believe me. We don't know how this kid did it. Usually it takes a riot squad to pull in that pair."

"You mean he didn't have any help?"

"Not according to the witnesses. We got the story from two witnesses who hang out in a poolroom near the alley where the fight took place. They said the kid did it all by himself. We check that neighborhood pretty close, and the patrol car just happened to pass by when it was all over. That right, Jim?"

The driver of the patrol car nodded. "That's right, sergeant. We saw the crowd up the alley and knew something was up. Wish we'd gotten there two minutes earlier," he added grimly. "The way it turned out though, the kid didn't need any help.

"The two witnesses said it started with another guy, and when this youngster tried to break it up, the two thugs turned on him. The other guy beat it. Never did find out who he was. He was smart enough to get out of there anyway."

Smith put his hand on Chip's shoulder, "You all right, Chip? You feel good enough to tell what happened?"

Chip nodded and ran the fingers of his left hand over the cut on his lip. "I can't talk too well," he said, smiling ruefully. "But that's about it. I tried to get away, but they wouldn't let me."

"But what started it? How'd you get mixed up in it?"

Chip hesitated and then continued, speaking slowly, "I don't know *what* started it, but the two men who jumped me were forcing a fight with someone else. When I tried to stop it, they ganged up on me. It was a case of fight or get beat up."

He stopped and attempted a smile, "Guess they did a pretty good job at that! Anyway, I gave them all I had."

"You can say that again, my boy," the officer said grimly. "All they could take!"

Smith turned to the desk sergeant. "What do we do now, sergeant? Are there any charges?"

TWO ON TWO, MINUS ONE

The sergeant shrugged his shoulders, "You don't have to do anything as far as we're concerned. This is a simple case of assault and battery. Those two will plead guilty, and we'll throw them in jail for a few months. Maybe they'll think a little more the next time. Mr. Hilton can go whenever he wants, but we'd like you to fill out this form for the record if you will, Mr. Smith."

Chip rose to his feet. "Let's get out of here," he said wryly. "I've seen all I ever want to see of those two."

"Young man," the officer replied, "I know they feel the same about you."

While Smith was talking with the sergeant, Solomon and Belding were helping Chip. Whittemore sidled in behind them and stood there without speaking. He was just as silent on the way home, but Solomon and Belding tried to get more details from Chip about the fight.

"You mean you don't know what the argument was about?" Solomon asked.

"No!" Chip said shortly.

"What did the other guy look like?" Belding asked.

"If it's OK," Chip said wearily, "I'd rather not talk anymore about it. I want to forget the whole thing."

"He must be some rat," Solomon said angrily, "running out after you saved him from a beating!"

A long silence followed, and the atmosphere in the car grew heavy. Chip felt sick and filled with a blank despondency. Now he knew! There was no longer a speck of doubt! Whittemore was a *coward*.

Chip glanced toward Bill Smith, who was driving steadily and had taken no part in the conversation. He wondered what the man was thinking about. Was it possible Smith knew the whole story? Chip's heart was heavy because of the humiliation he knew Whittemore had experienced—must be experiencing right now. After the fight, Chip had tried in vain to find an alibi to account for the desertion. How had Whittemore covered up all these years? There must have been a lot of times when the campers entrusted to his care had been in serious danger. Once again Smith's words came flashing back:

"I guess you've heard the old adage about the one bad apple in the barrel. Well, that applies to members of the staff as well as to campers."

CHAPTER 10

Running from the Block

BILL SMITH dropped Whittemore, Solomon, and Belding in front of the dining hall and then drove Chip over to his cabin. "You hop out and take it easy, Chip. I'll bring you something to eat. Guess you're not too keen on making a public appearance right now."

"Not the way I look," Chip said ruefully. "I'm not hungry, Mr. Smith."

Smith didn't argue the point, but he was back in a few minutes with hot soup, milk, and sandwiches. After Chip had eaten, Smith put aside the magazine he had been reading. "Want to tell me about it?" he asked abruptly.

Chip was at a loss for words. He was relieved when Smith continued. "You see, Chip, I've known all along Whittemore was mixed up in that fight. Not that I thought he started it. Oh, no! Not Whitty. But he'd be right in character running out on you after it started. You see, Chip, I know for a certainty what you probably only surmise. I know Whitty is a coward. I'm telling you this because I have a hunch you're confused. Right?"

Chip nodded gratefully, "I sure am, Coach Smith. It seems as if I get involved with Whittemore every time I turn around. I don't know why."

"You're not to blame, Chip. Whittemore is a peculiar boy. Cliff, Joel, Blaine, and I have tried to protect Whitty more or less from himself for several years. You see, Frank is all wrapped up in him and, well Frank Dodd's happiness means a lot to us. Beyond that, we've all felt there was a lot of good in Philip, and we've been hoping we could straighten him out. When I say *we,* it doesn't include Frank. It's beginning to look as though we've failed."

Smith's voice faltered, and he dropped his head. After a few seconds he said, "I don't suppose you've noticed it, but we've bolstered Whittemore's section with our strongest counselors. We've tried to pick the very best men we could get—all of them are qualified to handle a section as well as a cabin. We did that so the youngsters in Section D would have the maximum protection and leadership."

He rose from his chair and took a turn around the room before continuing. "No man likes to fall down where a boy is concerned, and that's another reason we've gone all out in trying to carry Phil. I admire the stand you took in protecting him this afternoon. Frankly, I don't think I could've been so kind."

Bill Smith resumed his pacing, and Chip tried to think of something to say. But he was confused and couldn't find the words to express his feelings. He was relieved when Smith spoke again.

"The camp season will be over in a week, and I guess we can cover Phil that long." He spread his hands in a gesture of resignation. "Then he'll be on his way to State, and Frank won't be hurt. You see, Chip, Frank knows nothing about this. That's the reason I'm going to ask you to do Cliff, Joel, Blaine, and me a big favor."

"I'll do anything I can, Mr. Smith. I'd like to help."

"Well, it will probably be awkward, but we'll be extremely grateful if you try to forget about the part Phil played in what happened this afternoon. Cliff, Joel, Blaine, and I have been hoping Phil might find himself as he grows a little older. By the time another summer rolls around, who can tell what will happen? Perhaps he'll snap out of it or get another job."

"I want to forget about this afternoon anyway, Mr. Smith. I wouldn't want anyone to know about it. Whittemore must have felt pretty bad at the police station. Coming back in the van, I thought Belding and Solomon would never stop talking about the fight. I wish I could help him."

Smith smiled. "I know," he said gently. "We all feel that way. Frankly, I think you can do more for Philip Whittemore than all the rest of us put together. Maybe you can help him when he gets to State. He's sure going to need an angel on his shoulder."

"I'd like to try," Chip said earnestly, "but he's pretty hard to get to know. For some reason, he doesn't like me."

"He might get over that, especially after this afternoon. You see, he realizes now that you know he's a coward. That might make a difference."

"It might," Chip agreed doubtfully, "but I wish it hadn't happened."

Smith changed the subject. "How much do you know about Cliff Burdette?" he asked abruptly.

"Not very much," Chip said slowly.

"Well," Smith said briskly, "I'm going to talk to him tonight about Whittemore and you. He's a fine man,

Chip, and he's something else. He's one of the finest psychologists in his profession. Right now, he's president of the National Association of College Psychologists and the head of the psychology department at Stratford College. You ought to know him better."

"I'd like to," Chip said simply.

"I'll see what I can do. See you in the morning, Chip. Good night."

It wasn't a good night for Chip. Smith had hardly closed the door before Jimmie and Frankie Dodd barged in, excitement written all over their faces.

"Wow! Look at *you!* What happened?"

"Solomon said you cleaned out the town all by yourself!"

"It's true, Frankie! We gotta publicize this!"

They were gone as swiftly as they had arrived, and Chip knew the story would be all over Camp All-America by morning. He could hear Jimmie: "Chip whipped the whole bunch! All by himself! The police have been trying to break up that gang for years, and Chip managed it all by himself in one afternoon! You see, it was like this . . ."

The next morning they were back. Right on the dot, at six o'clock. Every muscle in Chip's body ached. But he made it out to the football field and hit the track, and soon the knots and aches began to disappear.

Frank Dodd took one look at Chip's battered face and grinned, "What does the other guy look like?" However, he gave Chip no mercy, hustling him through the grass drill and kicking and passing for more than an hour. Whittemore didn't show up, and Chip was glad. He didn't want to face Whittemore just yet. Not until he had talked with Cliff Burdette.

Chip skipped breakfast, but Jimmie brought him some sandwiches and a carton of milk. Afterward, he went to the athletic office and found Cliff Burdette waiting. The camp director wasted no time in preliminaries.

"Bill told me what happened yesterday, Chip. You deserve a lot of credit. He also told me about his conversation with you last night. I'm not too sure it's fair to get you involved any further with Philip Whittemore. He's quite a handful at times."

"I know. I've discovered that, Mr. Burdette," Chip said quickly, "but if I can help, I'd like to do it."

"Well, we've tried to help him, but you might succeed where we've failed. Being mindful of ethical issues and avoiding technical jargon, it seems Whittemore has a block of some sort that is antagonized by certain situations or conditions. If someone could find out what causes this block, Philip might be helped. But it would be a tough job. Such blocks are not cleared away easily. I'm actually surprised, but pleased, he's found such success on the athletic field."

Chip learned a lot about psychology during the short half-hour. Burdette impressed upon him the difficulties, the perseverance, and the time that would be required to earn Whittemore's friendship and confidence.

"It will be an extremely confidential matter, Chip, just between Whittemore and you. If you succeed in finding the cause of this block—and that's going to be difficult—you will have to observe the strictest confidence, because Whittemore will have to trust you implicitly before he can be helped. Remember, he's undoubtedly deeply ashamed of his weakness. He will be reluctant to admit it, discuss it, or share it. It's a tough assignment for anyone. But maybe you'll succeed."

"I can try," Chip said earnestly. He was resolved to help Philip Whittemore if for no other reason than to repay the camp leaders, especially Frank Dodd, for all the things he had learned during the past seven weeks.

Jimmie Dodd was enjoying his supposedly secret knowledge of Chip's fight in town. He spent the whole morning moving from group to group, broadcasting the details. His travels brought him to Coach Don Kim and a stranger who was standing near the track beside an unfamiliar car. Jimmie wasn't going to overlook Don Kim.

He went right up to the convertible. "You hear about Chip?" he demanded, eyeing Kim curiously. "Hear about him cleaning out the bad guys? Put seven of them in the hospital!"

Kim grinned and nudged his companion. "Sure, I heard about it, Jimmie. I was just telling Mr. Carter here about it. Jimmie, do me a favor, will you? Send Whittemore down here. This gentleman wants to talk to him."

"Sure, Coach Kim!" Jimmie turned away, stopped, and suddenly pivoted. "What do you want to see him about?" he demanded.

"Oh, just something about school."

Later, watching Whittemore talking to Kim and the stranger, Jimmie had a presentiment. "Bet that man's a football coach," he muttered, studying the man's broad shoulders. "Bet he's from A & M. Humph! Guess Pop would want to know about this!"

Chip was still sensitive about his black eye and general appearance and had spent most of the day in the office. That's where Jimmie Dodd found him just before dinner. Jimmie was scowling, and his lips were pursed obstinately. He flopped down on a chair, folded his arms, and glared steadily at the floor.

"Well," Chip observed, "you're in one of those moods! Now what?"

"Whitty! He's going to A & M! Some guy from A & M visited Don Kim this morning, and he talked Whitty into it. Pop's all upset, sore at everybody. You gotta do something, Chip."

"Me?"

"Yes, you. Punch him in the jaw! Put him in the hospital. Throw him in the lake. Something! Anything! He's leaving this evening. This Carter guy is driving him home and then to A & M's football camp. Pop's mad enough now, but if Whitty leaves, he'll be impossible!"

"What makes you think I can do anything about it?"

"You can pop him in the nose, can't you?"

"That wouldn't solve anything. Maybe I can work it some other way. Tell you what I'll do. I'll give it a try if you give me your word of honor not to breathe it to a soul. Promise?"

That was good enough for Jimmie. He assured Chip it would be kept a secret as long as he lived. "Whitty's in his cabin right now," he whispered. "Packing! That guy Carter is down with Kim. Hurry, Chip."

Whittemore was packing, all right. In fact, he was already packed. Whitty opened the door when Chip knocked. He stood in the doorway facing Chip nervously. Behind him, a foot locker and two traveling bags were sitting in the center of the cabin.

"Mind if I come in?" Chip asked, moving through the doorway.

"What do you want?" Whittemore said shortly, recovering from his surprise.

Chip gestured toward the packed bags. "I heard you were leaving for home," he said calmly, "and I wanted to talk to you about State before you made a hurried decision."

Whittemore regarded Chip warily. "You wanted to talk to me about State?" he echoed. "Not about anything else?"

"Of course not. There's nothing else to talk about."

"I thought you might want to talk to me about—"

"About the fight? No," Chip said softly. "If we'd both tangled with those two crazies, the rest of that crowd might have joined in, and we'd have been in some real trouble.

"No, Whitty, I want to talk to you about State because I feel you may be considering A & M because of what happened yesterday. I wouldn't want that to happen."

Whittemore's attitude made it clear he was confused; he was finding it difficult to understand Chip's interest. Perplexed, he motioned Chip to a chair and sat down heavily on his bunk. "I don't understand," he said. "You mean *you* want me to go to State? After the way I've treated you this summer?"

"Of course I want you to go to State," Chip said quickly. "As far as anything that has happened this summer is concerned, well, I've already forgotten it. I want you to go to State because you're a good football player and because you and Mr. Dodd have been planning it for years."

There was a short silence, and then Chip really opened up his heart about State, explaining how it was a friendly school, academically strong, and that there was no pressure in athletics. "I'm working my way through school," he continued. "My boss is an alumni of State. He gives me time off for practice and games, and there are a lot of men in University just like him." Chip hesitated, then continued tentatively, "Maybe you don't have to work, but if you do, I'll help you get a job."

Whittemore suddenly erupted into action, springing to his feet and aiming a vicious kick at one of the bags. "You finished?" he demanded fiercely. "Well, if you are,

suppose you get out of here and let me have a little pri-
vacy." He crossed swiftly to the door and yanked it open.
"As far as a job is concerned, Hilton," he said bitterly, "I
don't have to work. And if I did, I wouldn't ask you to help
me. Get out and stay out!"

CHAPTER 11

The Inside Story

DREW CARTER sighed contentedly and glanced at the big athlete sitting beside him in the front seat of the convertible. Carter was satisfied with the day's work. All those times he had watched Whittemore during the past two years were paying off now, he told himself. He'd had lots of company. Practically every big-name college in the country had sent someone to look over Central Junior College's big end who won game after game and caught pass after pass even when surrounded by opponents.

Carter appraised Whittemore's big hands, hands that could cradle a football the way most athletes handle a baseball. "He seems like a modest kid," he mused, "but he acts as if he's worried about something. Guess I'd better stop and get him something to eat. Nothing like a big meal to cheer up a football player."

At the first sight of a restaurant along the interstate, Carter lifted his foot from the gas pedal, signaled, and pulled off at the next exit. "How about something to eat?"

he said pleasantly. "That'll give us a chance to get better acquainted."

Whittemore followed Carter to a seat in one of the booths along the wall of the restaurant and sat down opposite the husky coach. Try as he might, Whittemore couldn't forget the hurt in Frank Dodd's eyes when he had broken the news. He had been trying to convince himself ever since that moment that he was within his rights to choose any college in the country. He argued to himself that it was an athlete's exclusive decision when it came to planning his education.

Carter's voice broke through his thoughts, jarring him back to reality and the knowledge that the die had been cast. "How about a nice steak?"

Whittemore shook his head uncertainly. "No, thanks. I don't want to eat right now. Maybe just a glass of milk."

"Oh, go ahead. A steak is just what you need. Waiter, we'll have two steaks, and bring us a couple of shrimp cocktails. How about one large milk? And I'll have an iced tea."

Whittemore fingered his silverware and tried to still his conscience. Sure, he told himself, most of the money he had saved for college had come from his camp job. But so what? Hadn't he worked hard for it?

"It's hot in here," Whitty muttered. "Do you mind if I take a little walk, Mr. Carter? I don't feel so well."

"Sure, go right ahead. I'll tell the waiter to hold one of those steaks. Take your time. I don't like to rush a good dinner."

Philip Whittemore wasn't the only one who didn't feel like eating that night. Dinner at Camp All-America was dismal—not for the campers. Nothing slowed down those knife-and-fork champions. But the men who were

chiefly responsible for the excellence of the food at Camp
All-America just weren't interested. Frank Dodd didn't
show up at all. Burdette, Goldstein, Scott, and Smith
merely went through the motions of eating, chiefly
because it was part of the job.

Chip was served in his cabin by his best friend, but
no one would have suspected they were more than
acquaintances. Jimmie showed up with a big tray of food,
but he completely ruined the gesture by avoiding Chip's
eyes until he was leaving. The reproachful glance he cast
in Chip's direction would have broken anyone's heart.

After lights out, Chip walked slowly back to his cabin
and tried to get interested in a book. But it was no use.
His mind reverted to the thoughts flooding it ever since
the disastrous discussion in Whittemore's cabin. Chip
couldn't figure out what he had said to upset
Whittemore. He turned out the light and tried to go to
sleep, but it was no use. Tossing and turning, he played
an imaginary game of football, which he won by exciting
runs, spectacular passes, and fifty-yard field goals. But
sleep still evaded him. He gave up, turned on the light,
and began dressing. Maybe a long walk would help.

A sharp knock on the door shattered the stillness,
and Chip nearly jumped out of his socks. His heart was
beating like a drum when he opened the door and saw
Whittemore standing on the porch. "Where'd you come
from?" he asked. "How'd you get here?"

"Dalesburg," Whittemore answered grimly. "I
walked."

"Walked? Why, that's almost twenty miles!"

"I know," Whittemore said quietly. "Can I come in?"

"Of course. Sure! I thought you went home."

Whittemore nodded. "I started," he said, dropping
down on a chair and studying his dusty shoes. After a

second he looked up and plunged in. "I couldn't do it, Chip. Just couldn't! Frank's been too good to me. I guess you're wondering why I'm here. Well, I want to apologize to you for this afternoon. I don't know why you didn't knock my block off. I never met anyone like you, Chip. You're not vindictive, and you don't hold a grudge. I guess that's the real reason I'm here."

"That didn't mean anything," Chip protested.

"Yes, it did," Whittemore said despondently. "You were trying to help me, and I was unapproachable and impossible." He sighed deeply and cleared his throat before continuing, obviously with an effort. "I was pretty angry this afternoon, Chip, angry because you acted as if you thought I was a coward."

Whittemore paused and breathed another deep sigh. "Well, you're right," he said hopelessly. "I *am* a coward! I'm afraid, and I can't do a thing about it!"

Chip didn't know what to say, and he didn't know how to break the long silence that followed. There was no doubt about the depth of Whittemore's emotion. Chip could almost feel the tension forcing Whittemore to make his confession. He started to speak, but Whittemore lifted his hand. "Let me finish, Chip." Then, haltingly, in a low and intense voice, Whittemore told his tragic story.

It was a long story that took place when Whittemore was twelve years old. It had haunted him ever since. The story was of a boy who had just learned to swim and who was practicing his new skill off the lonely beach of a seashore resort. The beach was deserted, with the exception of a girl swimming some distance away. She got caught in an undertow and screamed for help.

She was being carried out to sea, and Whittemore had been paralyzed with fear. Somehow, he managed to swim to shore, hoping to get help, but when he reached the beach, the cries for help had ceased and the girl was not in sight. He had been so ashamed that he never said anything about the incident to anyone, ever. But he had carried the painful wound in his heart ever since. Emergencies of any kind paralyzed him now just as the first one had that day at Pleasant Harbor.

As Chip listened, he knew there was more to it than an act of physical cowardice. That first terrifying occasion, perhaps, but since then it must have been something psychological, something that, unless it was cured, would affect Whittemore as long as he lived.

All of Chip's bitterness vanished as he listened to Whitty's story. He was filled with a deep longing to help him. He learned Whittemore's mother was dead and that his father had moved to the West Coast and remarried. Other children and other responsibilities had made it difficult for his father to help Whittemore, and he had been on his own for several years. The money he had saved and the help he could get through his athletic ability and a job were all he could count on for an education.

"All my trouble goes back to that day at the seashore, Chip. I know it, but I can't do anything about it. When faced with an emergency, I freeze up. I feel as though I'm paralyzed, the way a person feels when he's having a nightmare and can't move. It's terrible."

Chip's thoughts went back to his talk with Cliff Burdette. Now that Whittemore had revealed the cause of the mental block, there was some hope. "Things will work out," he assured Whittemore. "Wait and see."

"I don't think so, Chip. I've always been too ashamed to talk about it. Sometimes I get so discouraged I don't know what to do. I guess that's why I'm so mean to everyone. I've got to whip this thing, Chip. Maybe you can help me."

Whittemore shook his head. "How you can have anything to do with me after the way I've acted is beyond me," he said. "You're the most unselfish person I've ever met—keeping quiet after I left you to face those two guys in the alley and then not saying a word about it."

"I told you to forget that, Whitty. It's not important now."

"It's the most important thing that ever happened to me, Chip. It made me believe in people, people like you anyway. You're the first person I've met that I felt I could trust all the way. As much as I respect and admire Frank Dodd, I never could bring myself to destroy his confidence in me. If you can help me, I'll never forget it."

"I'll try," Chip said simply.

"And, Chip," Whittemore said haltingly, "please don't tell anyone what I've told you tonight."

Chip smiled with empathy, "You don't have to worry about that. But you'll have to tell someone who's qualified to help you. Hey, what did Carter say when you left?"

"He didn't know I was leaving, Chip. I just walked out. I've always walked or run out on things I didn't like, since—well, since that day at Pleasant Harbor. I called him on the phone though and told him I'd changed my mind."

"How did he take that?"

Whittemore grinned wearily, "Not too bad. He said he'd leave my stuff at the restaurant and if I changed my mind to let him know."

"You won't do that," Chip said firmly. "You're going to State! Let's go get your things. Come on. We'll ask Mr. Dodd for the pickup. It will give you a chance to tell him it was all a big mistake. Let's go!"

Chip never knew what Whittemore said to Frank Dodd, but they got the truck, and Whittemore was whistling softly when they turned onto the highway and headed for Dalesburg. Once they were underway, Whittemore opened up about the lake accident and the incident on the cliff when he claimed he'd injured his wrist.

"I didn't have a cramp that day on the lake, Chip, and I didn't hurt my wrist at Bear Mountain," he said in a low, ashamed voice. "Another thing. You remember the night of the storm? Well, I wasn't hit by lightning; I was afraid. I hid in my cabin closet like the coward I am."

Chip stopped him. "Listen, Whitty. That's all in the past. Let's talk about the future. We'll whip this thing together. That's a promise."

"There is one other thing, Chip. I lied to Cliff Burdette and Frank about Dan Pryor too. Dan was right. I did promise to take over for him when he went to the party. I should have been fired along with him."

"We'll make up for that some way," Chip said.

During Whittemore's story, the antagonism that had separated the two young men vanished. Now they seemed bonded together as closely as lifelong friends. They rode in silence, enjoying the wordless communion that graces true friendship.

Chip was involved in his new problem. He now knew the real-life trauma that Coach Burdette had explained. But the counseling Whitty needed was far beyond Chip's abilities. He felt bound by the promise he had made to Whittemore and was determined to keep that promise. But he also knew Whitty had to talk to Cliff Burdette or someone like him. Chip's thoughts ranged back to football. How could Whitty have played such good football if he was afraid? Why, he had been a junior college all-American selection.

Coincidentally, just as if he had read Chip's thoughts, Whittemore began to talk about football. "I guess you're wondering why I played football. It wasn't easy, but it meant tuition, books, and school fees. Luckily for me, the coach thought I was too valuable to play defense." He grunted ironically. "That's a laugh, isn't it?

"Anyway, when we had the ball, he played me outside as a flanker where I didn't have to do any blocking. When we were on the defense, he used me in the safety position. I made a lot of interceptions back there. When the other team kicked and I could see a little daylight, I'd run like crazy to keep from getting hit. And when it looked like the tacklers would cream me, I signaled for a fair catch."

"You're not a coward, Whitty," Chip said aggressively. "You couldn't be and talk as you have tonight. There's an explanation for all this. Some kind of explanation, and it's up to us to find it."

Things moved fast at Camp All-America after that eventful night. The days passed swiftly, too swiftly for Jimmie and Frankie. They worked feverishly at football and moaned and groaned about books and school and haircuts and new clothes and certain teachers who should have been bus drivers and vice versa.

Closing day arrived all too soon; the parking lot was filled with cars, and parents were all over the place. The pageant was beautiful, and as always, Philip Whittemore's diving was the climax to the waterfront show, summer friendships, and the season.

Camp was over.

As the cars and buses carried their passengers away from Camp All-America, many hearts were filled with the sadness that always comes at parting time and the end of a happy summer.

Jimmie and Frankie shadowed Chip every second of those last days, strangely quiet, their spirits dampened by the shadow of summer good-byes. But Jimmie made sure Chip and Whitty had a lift to New York City. And he managed to say good-bye to Whittemore when he learned Whitty was going home with Chip for a few days before reporting to State's football training camp at a place they called Camp Sundown. As the car passed under the red-white-and-blue wooden arch of Camp All-America, Jimmie and Frankie waved, and Jimmie shouted, "Dad says we'll be up for the first game, Chip. You better be the starting quarterback! And, Whitty, you better be on the receiving end of Chip's passes!"

CHAPTER 12

A Good Deception

CHIP PULLED his carry-on from the overhead bin as the plane's engines shut down at the Valley Falls airport. Home at last! Whittemore followed Chip down the aisle and up the jetway, his curiosity aroused by Chip's obvious excitement.

At the arrival gate, crowding right up to the doorway, were Chip's hometown friends. Before he knew it, his pals were all around him, slapping him on the back, pushing, hugging, laughing, and joking, all trying to shake his hand at the same time. They were all there. Soapy Smith, Biggie Cohen, Speed Morris, Red Schwartz, Joel Ohlsen, Tug Rankin, and Taps Browning. The Hilton Athletic Club was almost intact.

Then, just as if it had been rehearsed, a lane opened through the crowd, and there at the back stood Mary Hilton, smiling a mom's welcome. Chip's heart tightened as he lifted her up and spun her around with a giant hug. Then he introduced Philip Whittemore, and the whole crew piled into the waiting cars and headed to the Hilton residence, the home of the Hilton A. C.

After Soapy said he couldn't eat another bite—but did anyway—the crowd began reliving fond memories of the Hilton A. C. As the evening wore on, some said their good nights, and Hoops, the Hilton family cat, escorted each one down the hallway to the door. Those who remained joined Mrs. Hilton and Chip in the family room for more special memories.

This camaraderie was a new and enlightening experience for Philip Whittemore. Small-town stuff, and on the basis of first impressions, somewhat on the juvenile side. But as the week passed, he began to realize it wasn't kid stuff at all. It was something real and important to these guys, and he began to appreciate that he was privileged to observe the very foundations of their lifetime friendships.

Almost every night the guys ended up at Chip's home. Whittemore was amazed by Mary Hilton's gracious hospitality and personal interest in each of Chip's friends. After the Sugar Bowl closed, Petey Jackson would show up with ice cream and proceed to take the leading role in that night's session.

A great deal of the talk was serious. Whittemore learned Soapy Smith was about to give up his plans for a teaching career. "I think I should study law," Soapy said seriously. Then, unable to pass up a joke even if it was on himself, he added, "Got to do something with the gift of gab I've inherited."

Biggie Cohen was already pointing his study and outside reading toward engineering. Strange as it seemed to Whittemore, Joel Ohlsen, whose father owned practically the whole town, including its biggest industry, the pottery, was interested in medicine. The others had secret ambitions, that is, secret to everyone except their families and these close friends.

Saturday came all too soon for Chip. But a new varsity hopeful—especially a sophomore—didn't dare report late for training camp. Speed Morris's reliable Mustang and Petey Jackson's Firebird idled bravely in Chip's driveway while Soapy, Red, Biggie, and Whitty tried to find room for their bags and other college treasures.

Soapy kept watching the corner, and when Joel Ohlsen appeared behind the wheel of his father's Cadillac, he shouted, "Come on!" Biggie and Red tore after him and piled in the car almost before Joel came to a stop.

Ohlsen was grinning. "I told you I'd be here," he chortled, "told Dad it was my duty as class president to get things set for the opening of school." He winked happily at Soapy. "I didn't tell him I was going by way of Camp Sundown, of course."

"Let's go!" Soapy bellowed. "What are we waiting for?"

"Chet Stewart!" Speed replied. "He just got back in town from vacation and wanted to see us before we took off to camp."

Soapy shouted approval. "What a break! The school board bozos finally wised up and hired him as the new head coach of football, basketball, and baseball!"

Stewart, Henry Rockwell's former assistant and now head coach at Valley Falls High, was late. A few minutes later, Coach Stewart jogged around the corner and was mobbed by his old high school players. Then they were on their way.

Chip and Whittemore had the back seat of Petey's green Firebird all to themselves. They made good time, considering Soapy's hunger stops, but it was dark when they arrived at Camp Sundown. Their arrival was announced to all in camp by Soapy.

The happy-go-lucky redhead barged into every cabin without knocking, notifying the occupants, veteran lettermen, scrubs, and aspiring sophomores that the backbone of State's varsity had arrived, and they could all sleep peacefully now. Rapping on door after door, Soapy covered the whole camp. He was exhausted by the time he reached the last cabin, but he was determined to make it one hundred percent. Soapy jerked the door open, startling the occupants with his dramatic entrance and deafening yell.

"Heads up, chumps! Ralston's worries are over—" Soapy choked off the last word and cast another frenzied glance at the shocked faces of Curly Ralston, Henry Rockwell, and Nik Nelson, his former freshman coach. Soapy was paralyzed with surprise and stood there with his mouth wide open, expecting the worst. The coaches threw back their heads and laughed, and Soapy, retreating in confusion, apologized profusely, softly closed the door, and hurried back to the Valley Falls cabin.

Soapy was subdued for the rest of the evening, snapping out of it only when Fred "Fireball" Finley, Eddie Anderson, "Silent" Joe Maxim, Stavros "Bebop" Leopoulos, and Rod "Diz" Dean barged in and nearly tore the cabin to pieces. The old freshman pals right in that cabin added up to a pretty fair football team, even though they were only sophomores.

By Monday morning at suit-up time for conditioning, there were nearly one hundred football players at Camp Sundown. Curly Ralston and his staff worked them as if the first game was four days away instead of over four weeks away. By six o'clock that afternoon, players were sinking gratefully to the ground at every opportunity.

A GOOD DECEPTION

Soapy moaned. "Isn't this supposed to be a holiday?"

For the first three days, Curly Ralston kept pouring it on, and Chip mentally thanked Frank Dodd over and over again for those six o'clock camp sessions. After the NCAA-required three-day conditioning period, grass drills, blocking sleds, tackling dummies, group contact work, chasing punts and passes, wind sprints, and signals occupied the morning and afternoon workouts. Strategy sessions and videos were the routine every night. There wasn't much horseplay after the chalk talks and film discussions. Even Soapy was subdued and ready for the sack. A few rookies even fell asleep watching the films.

Whittemore had moved to Tims Lansing's cabin, but he lined up beside Chip whenever it was possible. Chip's friends had taken Whittemore in stride, reserving judgment until they knew him better. All were at a loss to understand Chip's interest in the big receiver, but no one would have guessed it by their attitudes.

Two or three candidates dropped out voluntarily every day, and others were cut at the end of the week. All of the Valley Falls contingent survived the cut. Observers could almost figure out the varsity squad from the amount of attention given to the various candidates by members of the coaching staff.

It was obvious that Ralston was concerned about receivers. The inability of Wally Curtis and Larry Higgins to handle his famous passing patterns the previous year was common knowledge. Whittemore received a lot of attention. He was fast, big, and flashy, and it was uncanny the way he could twist his big body and pull in the aerials. Clearly he had impressed Curly Ralston. Whitty was accepted without reservation by the varsity veterans because of his friendship with Tims

Lansing, but his standoffish attitude off the field hurt his popularity.

The following week, visitors began to show up for the workouts: sportswriters, alumni, and a few fans. The team knew it was coming. The Wednesday morning workout was light: signals, practice kickoffs, and punting and passing. They knew it was coming that afternoon even before Ralston blasted his whistle and sent them to the showers. "Three-thirty!" he shouted. "Helmets and pads!"

Chip and his crew skipped the regular lunch, munching fruit and downing sports drinks instead, and rested until 2:30. They were the first ones suited up and on the field. But everyone was on the job at 3:30. After a fast limbering-up grass drill, Coach Ralston's whistle brought them hustling to circle him in the center of the field.

"All right, men," he said crisply, "we're going to have a ninety-minute, full-contact scrimmage with all action stopping on the whistle. This is not a practice game. That comes Saturday against the freshmen. Coach Rockwell and I will call the plays in the huddle.

"The offense for Team A will line up with Curtis and Higgins at the ends; Morgan and Carlson, tackles; McCarthy and Clark, guards; Brennan, center. Backs: Lansing, Cole, Gibbons, and Burk.

"The offense for Team B is Schwartz and Whittemore, ends; Cohen and Maxim, tackles; Anderson and Smith, guards; Leopoulos, center. Backs: Hilton, Morris, Roberts, and Finley.

"I'll handle Team A; Coach Rockwell will take Team B. All right, Hank, Team A will kick. You defend the south goal. No special teams yet. I want the linemen up front and ball handlers deep to receive the kickoffs." He turned to the remaining players. "The rest of you men report to Coach Nelson over by the bleachers. Brush up on the signals, Nik, and have them ready for quick substitutions. Let's go!"

Biggie Cohen nudged Chip as they followed Rockwell toward the south goal. "Bring back any memories?" he whispered.

Chip nodded. "And how! Every one of them."

Team B circled on the twenty, and Chip's thoughts went back to high school and all the times when Soapy, Biggie, Red, Speed, and he had gathered around their coach. Yes, he remembered, all right. One didn't forget a man like Rock.

"All right, team," Rockwell said, extending his hand for the team clasp, "Let's have some good blocking. We'll pass on the first down, Chip. Number 29, Whittemore's ball, buttonhook in the hole. Alternate on the fifty, right sideline. Everybody got it? All right, mow 'em down!"

As Chip turned out of the huddle, he caught sight of Whittemore's face. It was dead white, just like those other times at camp. Chip turned back and thumped him on the back. "C'mon, Whitty!" he said sharply. "This is it! OK? You can do it."

Whittemore nodded uncertainly. "I guess so," he managed to reply.

Seconds later, Chip was back on the ten in front of the goal. Whittemore and Rockwell and everyone else were forgotten now except the ball resting on the kicking tee fifty-five yards away. As he waited for the kickoff, Chip's heart was thumping as loud as a drum.

Ralston blasted the whistle, and tough Mike Brennan, State's veteran center and captain, started forward to boot the ball. It was a bad kick, slithering off Brennan's kicking toe and heading straight for Whittemore.

Chip breathed and dug upfield. "Whitty, hold that ball!" he shouted.

It was a fast, twisting kick, and the ball rose no higher than a man's shoulders. But fast as it was, the varsity tacklers were almost as fast and only a few steps behind, converging on the receiver. Whittemore couldn't have dropped the ball if he had wanted to; it plunked right into his arms and stuck there. But he wavered in the face of the hard-charging tacklers and then broke, turned, and ran to the rear, clutching the ball and looking desperately for a way to escape. The varsity tacklers changed direction and bore down on Whittemore just as Chip swept across the field behind him.

"Here, Whitty!" Chip cried. "Here! Lateral! Give me the ball!"

Whittemore passed the ball back toward Chip as though it were a hot potato and kept going, heading in the opposite direction and running for his life. Chip caught the ball without breaking stride and streaked for the sideline. A yard from the sideline stripe he changed direction and headed straight for the goal line seventy yards away. There was nothing but daylight ahead; it was a sure touchdown run. But Ralston's whistle brought him to a halt on the varsity forty.

"All right, all right!" Ralston barked. "First and ten here on the fifty. Nice work, Whittemore, Hilton. Good deception!"

CHAPTER 13

The Paper Offense

WHITTEMORE DUCKED into the huddle, giving Chip a quick, half-ashamed glance, shaking his head dejectedly. Chip grinned and winked with a nod of approval. "Beautiful, Whitty," he said warmly. "Nearly fooled *me*."

Rockwell started to say something to Whittemore, but Chip's words and attitude stopped him, and he let it slide, shaking his head skeptically. Rock didn't like runners who backtracked. He wanted his ball carriers to drive ahead and get all the yardage possible.

"Good start," Chip said enthusiastically, peering over the heads of his teammates at the varsity defense. "Nice blocking! Let's keep rolling. Play 29 now. Buttonhook in the hole. Your play, Whitty. Alternate pass is yours, Roberts. Right sideline, thirty-yard stripe. Ball on four. Let's go!"

Ralston's plays were set up with standard blocking assignments for a 4-3 defense. A shift from this defensive front alignment was countered by a check signal from the quarterback when his team reached the line of scrimmage. A code number was used to designate the blocking changes to meet the defensive shift.

Team A shifted into a 6-3-2 when Team B reached the scrimmage line, and Chip chuckled to himself. Just the ticket! Now he could fake Fireball into the middle of the line and decoy Speed and Schwartz into the flats to open up the secondary; the hole would be wide open for Whittemore.

Chip gave the check signal, paused, gave the code number for the 6-3-2 defense, and paused again. Then he counted for the charging signal in a sharp, vibrant voice.

"Hut one! Hut two!"

Pivoting swiftly, Chip faked the ball to Fireball driving into the center of the line and faked again to Speed Morris cutting out toward the right flat. Eddie Anderson and Soapy faked their charge, and then, timing their moves perfectly, dropped back to form the passing pocket. Two quick steps brought Chip into passing position. He saw Whittemore speeding downfield with long, fast strides.

Chip cocked his arm, faked the throw to Morris and, just as Whittemore buttonhooked, fired a bullet pass over the head of the middle linebacker. It was a baseball catcher's peg, hard and fast but higher in the air, and only a giant or a receiver with steel springs in his legs could have caught the ball.

Whittemore did it. He leaped high in the air, his arms stretched full length, and caught the spinning ball. He streaked toward the right sideline and picked up Morris for a blocker, and they were off. Speed cut Tims Lansing's feet out from under him with a perfectly timed block, and Whittemore was away. Ralston blasted the whistle to stop the speeding runner. But Whitty wasn't taking any chances. He didn't even look back until he crossed the goal line. It was such a beautiful catch that Ralston didn't have the heart to criticize the runner. Instead, he loosed his wrath upon the varsity defense.

"Two plays, two touchdowns!" he stormed. "Where's the pass defense? Where's the hustle in the line? What's wrong with rushing the passer?" He turned wrathfully on Brennan. "You're captain of this team," he said harshly. "You're calling the defense. What's wrong with these guys? Don't they want to play defense? Don't tell me I'll have to sit through another season and watch this team fall apart every time some cute quarterback mixes up his plays."

Ralston glared at Brennan a long second and then waved his hand in disgust. "All right. See what you can do with the ball. Take over on the twenty!"

Chip hadn't dared to move while Ralston was speaking. But now he hurried into the defensive huddle beside Speed Morris, anxious to try the plan he had worked out to overcome Whittemore's defensive weakness. "Trade places with me, Speed," he whispered. "Quick! It's important. Play safety."

Speed was surprised, but he didn't show it. He nodded in agreement, and when the huddle broke, he trotted back to the safety position. Chip took Speed's defensive left halfback position behind Whittemore. Directly ahead, in the left tackle slot, Biggie Cohen was resting on one knee, his broad back a comforting bulwark of strength. Fireball Finley stood behind Biggie with his hands on his hips, a picture of a hungry tackler.

Chip liked what he saw ahead of him. Cohen stood six-four and carried 240 pounds of devastating fury. Fireball was an even six feet in height and could shift his 210 pounds of muscle with the speed of a mongoose. He was all man and a deadly tackler. Whittemore was in first-class football company.

At first glance, Whittemore and Biggie Cohen looked like clones. But an observer dropped that thought fast when he noticed Biggie's large neck, massive shoulders, and hamlike hands. Biggie was thirty pounds heavier, hard as steel, and as fast as a scatback. Chip grinned. Maybe it would work.

But Chip hadn't taken the coaching staff into consideration. Rockwell sauntered over from his position behind the defensive line. "What's the idea?" he drawled. "How come you're up here?"

"Just a little experiment, Coach," Chip said quickly. "I want to show Biggie up. I'm going to make all the tackles on this side of the line."

"Oh, yeah?" Biggie challenged. "We'll see about that!"

Fireball swung suddenly around and glared at Chip. "What is this?" he demanded, feigning anger. "A two-man team? Maybe Anderson and Whittemore and one Fireball Finley will have a hand in that! Right, Eddie? Right, Whittemore? Humph!"

Most teams run better to the right. Perhaps it's because most people are right-handed. Tims Lansing sized up Team B's line, particularly Biggie Cohen. He wanted to test Cohen. At any rate, Team A's first play was a tackle smash over Cohen.

It turned out to be an *attempted* tackle smash. Biggie threw the blockers aside like bags of flour and broke through the line as though it was paper. He met Buzz Burk head on and carried him back five yards before he flattened him on the grass.

The ball flew out of Burk's arms, and Fireball Finley grabbed it with a shout of joy. Ralston's whistle stopped Fireball, and he tossed the ball to the ground. Burk was gasping for breath when he crawled to his feet, but he had time to give Bill Carlson and Dex Clark a long, questioning look. "Blockers?" he muttered sarcastically.

Biggie and Fireball swaggered back to their positions, grinning and gleefully nudging each other in the ribs. "He's gonna make *all* the tackles," Biggie said, nodding toward Chip.

"That's what the man *said*," Fireball chuckled.

Larry Higgins had used a reverse shoulder block to force Whittemore cleanly out of the play, but only Chip noticed it. Tims Lansing must have thought of Whittemore's defensive weakness then, for he started speedy Boots Cole around Whitty's end on the very next play. It was an in-and-out sweep, but Fireball Finley broke past two would-be blockers and chased Boots back ten yards before he dropped him with a crash that could be heard clear across the field. Chip had tried to get in on that one but didn't have a chance.

Fireball lifted Cole to his feet with exaggerated politeness and patted him on the back. "Tell Lansing to try the other side of the line," he suggested. "Nobody, but nobody, is going to get anywhere on this side."

Lansing tried a pass on the next down, but Junior Roberts knocked it down. The veterans were desperate now. After several attempts, they were able to eke out a first down with quick opening plays over Joe Maxim and Eddie Anderson. Bebop Leopoulos, backing up that side of the line, made the tackles after short gains.

That was the way it went all through the scrimmage. Team A couldn't do a thing in the air, and its ground game was limited to a few short gains over left tackle and around the left end. The Team A players did tighten up defensively against Team B's running game, but they couldn't stop Chip's passes. He hit Morris, Roberts, Schwartz, and Whittemore with his tosses time after time.

TEN SECONDS TO PLAY!

That night, after the inevitable skull practice, Chip and friends reviewed the scrimmage. They were pleased with their showing, but Soapy was obnoxiously boastful. "We killed 'em!" he exulted. "Killed Ralston's varsity and Ralston too!"

"That was this afternoon," Biggie reminded Soapy. "Don't underestimate players like Brennan, Morgan, and McCarthy. They'll get going."

"They're all linemen," Eddie Anderson observed. "It's my guess Ralston will be making some changes in his backfield, and soon!"

While this discussion was going on, Chip was sitting at the cabin's only table, thoughtfully writing on a piece of paper the names of the veterans and those of his sophomore friends who were vying for the same position. He evaluated each player carefully, eliminating all except the two best for each position on offense, and placed their names side by side. When he finished this preliminary task, he went down the list of names again and wrote the player he considered superior in a third column. This column was headed "Starters."

	Vets			Sophs			Starters
LE	Curtis	6-3	198	Whittemore	6-4	210	Whittemore
LT	Morgan	6-4	190	Cohen	6-4	240	Cohen
LG	McCarthy	5-11	245	Anderson	5-9	185	McCarthy
C	Brennan	6-0	205	Leopoulos	6-2	190	Brennan
RG	Clark	5-8	180	Smith	6-0	200	Smith
RT	Carlson	6-2	188	Maxim	6-2	195	Maxim
RE	Higgins	6-5	180	Schwartz	5-11	175	Higgins
QB	Lansing	6-1	180	Hilton	6-4	185	x
LH	Cole	5-11	165	Morris	5-11	170	Morris
FB	Gibbons	6-0	200	Finley	6-0	210	Finley
RH	Burk	5-9	170	Roberts	6-3	230	Burk

THE PAPER OFFENSE

Chip took a long time deciding between Whittemore and Wally Curtis. They were about the same size, but Whitty was much faster, and there was no comparison when it came to pulling in the passes. If—and Chip realized it was a big question mark—if the defense plan he had tried that afternoon worked as well in the future, Whitty was the man. Since Coach Ralston was going to platoon his squad, Curtis and Whittemore would make a wonderful combination because Wally was the reckless, crashing type of defensive end Ralston liked. But Chip also knew some of the players would play a lot of downs on offense and defense.

Choosing Biggie Cohen over Joe "Troubles" Morgan was easy. Biggie got the job because he was bigger, faster, stronger and better in every department of line play. He was undoubtedly the best lineman on the squad, perhaps in the whole country. Biggie would probably play both sides of the line.

Eddie Anderson was fast and had a lot of guts, but "Tiny Tim" McCarthy was nearly as fast and much more experienced. Tiny was a tough middleman in a five-man defensive line. McCarthy got the nod.

Chip didn't hesitate when it came to the center spot. Brennan was an expert center: big, fast, aggressive, tough, and a good captain—better all around than Bebop Leopoulos. "He belongs," Chip assured himself, "belongs on any man's team!"

Soapy moved in front of Dex Clark for several reasons. Soapy was fast, smart, a hustling fighter who never gave up, win or lose. He played offense or defense and could pull out of the line to block or run interference like a halfback. "I'm for Soapy," Chip muttered grimly.

When it came to the other tackle position, there was little to compare between Silent Joe Maxim and Bill

Carlson. But Silent Joe was the tougher competitor; he liked it best when the going was tough, and he backed up for no man. Silent Joe had to be the choice.

Chip reluctantly gave Larry Higgins the bid over Red Schwartz. Higgins was bigger, faster, and more experienced. Furthermore, he was potentially a great pass receiver. Larry had wonderful hands and could go up a mile to pull down a pass. Chip liked tall, rangy ends. It would have to be Larry to team up with Whitty.

Chip bent over backward when it came to a comparison between Tims Lansing and himself. Tims had two years of varsity-game experience, but Chip knew he himself to be faster and a harder runner, by far the better passer and kicker and as good defensively. "I'll just leave that position open," he decided. "Let's wait and see what happens."

When it came to the halfback positions, Chip selected Speed Morris and Buzz Burk over Boots Cole and Junior Roberts. Speed and Buzz were lightning fast, took off like jets when driving into the line or around end, and each speedster could turn on a dime. Defensively, they were outstanding.

Last but not least, Chip considered the fullbacks. Physically, Ace Gibbons and Fireball Finley might have been made in the same mold. Both were six feet in height. Ace balanced the scales at an even 200 pounds; Fireball went ten pounds heavier. Each could crack a line like a mad stallion, and each was a fearless competitor. There was little to distinquish between the two, but Fireball was faster. Chip went with Fireball.

"That's it," he mused, folding the paper and placing it in his pocket. "Now to get some sleep."

CHAPTER 14

Hungry Sophomores

CURLY RALSTON had trouble getting to sleep that night. Every practice and every scrimmage brought clear-cut evidence that State's coaching staff, and he in particular, had a problem. Football fans, no doubt, would wonder what sort of problem a coach could possibly have with a veteran team back intact from the previous season and reinforced by a bunch of talented sophomores. *That* was the point. The newcomers, the sophomores, were demonstrating time after time and in every department of the game that the veteran lettermen should be backing up the sophomores. And that was the problem!

State's alumni, student body, sportswriters, and every fan in the state were looking forward to a sensational season because an all-veteran team would be taking up where it had left off the preceding year. As the days began to get crisper and shorter, old grads and fans everywhere began to talk football.

State's followers were exceptionally jubilant. They bragged about the defensive abilities of State's forward wall: blocks of concrete like Troubles Morgan, tough Mike Brennan, Tiny Tim McCarthy, Dex Clark, and Bill "Swede" Carlson; the pass-receiving talents of rangy Wally Curtis and skyscraper Larry Higgins; the deceptive ballhandling of Tims Lansing; the block-busting rushes of Ace Gibbons and the breathtaking speed of Buzz Burk and Boots Cole.

State's coaching staff heard the rumors and read the papers and smiled and listened and yessed everybody and went to bed every night worried sick. Ralston had been exposed to this type of big-time football pressure for many years and summed it up best. "We haven't played a game yet, but we're undefeated! We've won the conference championship without making a touchdown, and we've just been invited to compete in the greatest post-season game in football before the Rose Bowl Selection Committee has had its first meeting since last New Year's Day! Oh, sure!"

"Yes," Rockwell added, "you've been named Coach of the Year and given a twenty-year contract! And Nik and I are riding around in new sports cars—gifts from admiring fans. You know something? I've never had a sports car!"

Nik Nelson grunted. "Humph! I never even rode in one! Curly," he said pointedly, "you've got yourself a problem."

Ralston grinned, "You mean we've got a problem."

It really was Ralston's problem. It is always the job of the head coach to make the decisions. His assistants usually suffer with him when the wolves begin to howl or share in his success when the salary increases, new job openings or contracts are handed out.

Yes, it was Ralston's problem. He knew it and so did his assistants. They stood ready to help, of course. But the coaching principles, philosophies of attack and defense, scouting information desired, and final decisions with respect to players were his responsibilities. A strong man likes it that way. Coach Curly Ralston was a strong man.

So Curly Ralston spent more sleepless nights trying to decide whether to break up a veteran team and build one around the flashy sophomores, or to stand by last year's lineup and risk everything on the basis of experience, or, based on the depth charting the coaches had been doing, select some of the veterans and sophomores in a new combination on offensive and defensive.

Ralston didn't doubt the value of that old football axiom, "A team is as good as its bench." But the heart and courage of every championship team rests in the hands of key performers and perfect team play—as demonstrated by Brown University's Eleven Iron Men, Fordham's Seven Blocks of Granite, and Notre Dame's Four Horsemen. These great teams had key players, all right. But they had something more. They had split-second timing, perfect team coordination, spirit, drive, and key players who wanted to be in there every minute of every game.

Ralston had something else to think about. One of his pet football philosophies was the one he repeated often when talking to veteran players or aspiring candidates: "The best man gets the job!"

Coach Ralston believed in that principle. It meant there was always keen competition for every position on the team. If a player was good, the constant banging away of a challenger kept him on his toes. If two candidates were of equal ability, the one who fought a little harder, practiced a little longer, and had the keener desire to win got the call. If it was impossible to choose one over the other, he could send one in and pull the other. If the one who went in didn't deliver, he could yank him and send the first one back.

The principle kept a squad on its toes—it kept every man fighting for a job and gave the coach a fighting, scrambling team of never-say-die hustlers who fought like wildcats all week to start each game and then fought like Tasmanian devils to stay out on the field.

Ralston understood that a player didn't develop offensive or defensive smoothness and timing in a week or even a couple of weeks, not when the players were new to one another and to the coach's style of play. It takes time. A few teams master it during the preseason training. Others develop it after game experience, while some require a season or two before it is perfected. Ralston knew it would be folly to wait much longer if he was going to go with the sophomores. He decided to wait until after the annual scrimmage game with the freshman squad.

Saturday turned out to be a perfect football day. It was cool with enough sun to brighten the blue-gray sky. Chip was sitting between Biggie Cohen and Soapy Smith when the officials stationed themselves on the field, and the veteran starters aligned at the thirty-five-yard stripe for the kickoff. He had been sizing up the freshmen during the warm-up, remembering his feelings from a year ago and trying to determine whether this year's crop was as strong as the one that had reported the previous August at Camp Sundown.

Captain Mike Brennan poised for the kickoff, started slowly forward, and then picked up speed, kicking the ball with a resounding thump that sent the pigskin high in the air, end over end, and down to the freshman ten.

The game was on!

HUNGRY SOPHOMORES

The freshman receiver barely made it to the twenty before he was buried under a swarm of tacklers. The veterans looked good on that one. They had sprinted through and around the freshmen blockers as if they were tender stalks of corn. Then they proceeded to crush the freshman attack before it could get started, forcing the yearlings back to the fifteen-yard line in three downs.

The freshman fullback punted to Lansing at midfield, and Tims ran it back to the freshman thirty. A smash into the line by Ace Gibbons was good for seven. Boots Cole made it a first down on the sixteen by spinning around end behind perfect blocking, and Lansing whipped a pass over the line to Higgins that was good for twelve and advanced the ball to the freshman four-yard line. It was another first down, goal to go, and the freshmen called time.

The time-out didn't help. Lansing faked to Buzz Burk cutting inside tackle and slipped the ball to Ace Gibbons on a cross buck. The veteran fullback smashed through the right guard for the touchdown and booted a perfect placement for the extra point. It was as easy as that!

The freshmen elected to receive again, tried the line with no gain, and attempted a pass. Lansing intercepted and scampered forty yards for another touchdown. Gibbons again booted the placement between the uprights.

Changing tactics, the freshman chose to kick following that tally. The result was plain murder. Cole took the kickoff boot, picked up good blocking, and went all the way to the freshman thirty-five before the kicker dropped him. Then the varsity took just four running plays to chalk up its third touchdown in seven minutes of play. It was no contest.

Ralston substituted the sophomores at that point, and it got worse. Chip booted the ball to the freshman goal line and Fireball Finley hit the receiver so hard he fumbled the ball. Soapy Smith fell on the ball on the seven-yard line, and it was first down, goal to go. Finley went all the way, taking the ball from Chip on a straight buck over the middle; he scored standing up. Chip booted a perfect placement. The first quarter ended after the tally with the score Varsity 28, Freshmen 0.

The veterans came back at the start of the second quarter and tallied four touchdowns, striking swiftly for a score every time they got the ball. Tims Lansing was in on three of the touchdowns, firing a forty-yard pass to towering Larry Higgins in the end zone for the first. Lansing scored the second after intercepting a pass on his own forty and racing all the way. Then, with the ball on the freshman thirty-eight, Tims started around left end on a fake pitchout, kept the ball, and raced down the left sideline for another touchdown.

The veterans added further to the humiliation of the State novices by blocking a punt on the freshman ten. Tiny McCarthy fell on the ball in the end zone for the touchdown. Ace Gibbons kicked all four extra points. That made the score Varsity 56, Freshman 0. Ralston called off the game then and sent both teams to the showers.

It was Saturday night and it had been a long week, but that meant nothing to Curly Ralston. He believed in saturating his players with football during training camp and prior to the first game. Thereafter, scrimmages and evening skull sessions were infrequent.

There wasn't much joy in Chip's cabin that night. In fact, the gloom was so thick that Soapy Smith's jokes fell flat, and after several futile attempts to cheer up his pals, the happy-go-lucky funster gave up and got serious. "Looks as if you were right about Brennan and those guys, Biggie," he said, elbowing his way to a seat on the bunk between Cohen and Finley. "They looked like a million bucks this afternoon," he added glumly.

"Who wouldn't?" Fireball demanded. "That wasn't a university football team; it was more like a cheering squad."

"Maybe so," Chip observed, "but fifty-six points in two quarters takes a lot of doing."

"One thing is sure," Schwartz added darkly, "the coach isn't going to break up the varsity after that exhibition. You heard all that yelling from the sidelines. Well, the guys doing all that cheering were the alumni."

"Yeah," Soapy added sarcastically, "and they think those guys are the greatest since the Four Horsemen! Probably got Ralston thinking the same thing."

"Uh-uh," Fireball remonstrated. "Ralston's no fool. He knows the freshmen were a pushover. That's why he called the game. We'll get another chance, and when we do—"

Peculiarly enough, right at that moment, Ralston and the members of his staff were discussing the advisability of another freshman-varsity scrimmage. "That's the worst freshman team I ever saw," Curly observed bitterly. "Absolutely the poorest material. Oh, what's the use?"

"Maybe we're better than we figured," Nelson ventured.

"No," Ralston said, shaking his head decisively. "I'm afraid not. Well, I'll figure something out tomorrow. Talking isn't going to help."

Ralston figured out something but said nothing to his associates or to the players until after skull practice

Tuesday night. "We're taking a little trip tomorrow morning," he announced before dismissing the squad. "I'll expect everyone to have full game equipment and be at the tennis court at eight o'clock. We'll be back tomorrow night. That's all." The team headed for the door but slowed down when Ralston added significantly, "Get a good night's rest."

Two buses were waiting at the tennis court the next morning, and at 8:15 sharp, they pulled away from Camp Sundown and drilled steadily north on the interstate.

"Lake Michigan," someone whispered hoarsely. "Western's training up there somewhere."

"A scrimmage game," another added. "Tough team!"

"Yeah, played in the Sugar Bowl last New Year's Day. And everyone's back!"

"So what! We beat them the year before last. Beat them bad. We'll do it again."

"How come we don't play them this year?"

"State's only allowed two nonconference games, remember? We've got Southwestern and the Dukes this year."

The grapevine was right. It was eleven o'clock when the two buses turned off the highway and followed the road to a camp that might well have been Camp Sundown but for the location. They were greeted jovially by the entire Western squad, with a variety of remarks.

"Long way to come to get your butts beat!"

"Where's the varsity? How come they sent you guys?"

That was too much for Soapy. "Coach didn't want to ruin your season!" he yelled. "You guys all cheerleaders?"

Western probably had a fine squad of cheerleaders, but they weren't on hand that afternoon at two o'clock when Ralston sent his veterans out to receive the kickoff. The team that lined up to boot the ball downfield to State's veterans was the same team that had won the Sugar Bowl and completed an undefeated season the previous year. There was one substitution for State; Philip Whittemore was at left end in place of Wally Curtis.

CHAPTER 15

Caught Asleep!

HENRY ROCKWELL had been playing and coaching football for many years. He was twenty years Curly Ralston's senior and qualified in every respect to be a head football coach for any university. But Rock had scaled the heights and had no aspirations other than the opportunity to contribute to the training and education of the present generation. Dr. D. H. "Dad" Young, State's director of athletics, had hired Rockwell after the veteran coach retired from his position as head coach of football, basketball, and baseball at Valley Falls High School.

Rock's original assignment had been to coach State's freshman teams because of his know-how, years of experience, and understanding of young athletes. But Curly Ralston also knew a good thing when he saw it and practically threatened to resign if Rockwell was not assigned to be his first assistant. Since Young was solidly in Ralston's corner, he reluctantly consented. As Ralston's first assistant, Rockwell was not concerned with the overall responsibility of handling the team and could concentrate on the players instead of the action.

Philip Whittemore looked like the answer to a coach's prayer. He was big, fast, and could pull in the passes. Ralston was counting on the impressive junior college graduate to hold down left end, but Henry Rockwell was dubious; he had noticed Whittemore's reluctance to go all out when it came to blocking and tackling. Now, as Rock watched State line up to receive the kick, his thoughts went back to the scrimmage episodes when Whittemore had quit cold.

"We'll soon know," Rockwell muttered, remembering several of his former players who had looked bad in practice but had been bearcats in the regular games. He focused his attention on the big end and hoped for the best.

Chip had been surprised, almost shocked, when Ralston named Whittemore as a starter. Whitty's face had taken on that white, scared look Chip had come to know, and he had thrown a quick, nervous glance in Chip's direction. In the huddle Chip gave him a vigorous thump on the back, whispered good luck, and then wedged himself between Soapy and Biggie. He paid little attention to the conversation of his friends at first, but it was impossible to ignore Soapy very long.

"How come?" Soapy demanded, elbowing Chip and jerking his head toward the field. "Whittemore!"

"I don't know, Soapy."

"You ever see him make a tackle?"

"What's your point?"

Soapy ignored the question and persisted with his own. "Ever see him throw a block?"

Just then, Western kicked off, and Chip concentrated on the game. It was a good boot and carried to the goal line where Tims Lansing gathered it in and headed toward the center of the wedge. Whittemore cut to his right a little ahead of Lansing but apparently failed to see Western's right guard drive swiftly past him to drop Tims with a vicious tackle on the fifteen-yard line.

"See that?" Soapy growled, digging his elbow into Chip's ribs. "He didn't even try!"

Lansing sent Ace Gibbons crashing into the middle, but the Western line didn't give an inch. On the next play, Tims whipped a pass over the line to Whittemore after faking to Buzz Burk. It was a good fake and a good pass, and Whittemore should have had it. He got his hands on the ball, but a Western back leaped with him— not quite as high, but still high enough.

The ball bounded in the air and into the hands of Western's alert cornerback. Tiny McCarthy dropped him almost as soon as he caught the ball, but the damage was done. It was Western's ball on State's eighteen-yard line, first and ten.

Western came out of the huddle and into a box formation, shifted right to a single wing, and smashed outside tackle. Whittemore came across the line too fast and too far, and Western's running guard didn't even bother to chase him. He, instead, turned in and threw a perfect block on Mike Brennan. Troubles Morgan was hit by Western's right tackle and right end and didn't have a chance. Boots Cole brought the ball carrier down on the seven-yard line, and it was first and goal. After a thrust into the line for three and a sweep around Whittemore, Western had its touchdown.

Whittemore had faced the screen of blockers on the sweep and dropped down on all fours. The interferers sped past him, and Whitty could have reached out and brought the runner down easily. But he didn't make the try. It was a disgraceful performance.

CAUGHT ASLEEP!

Chip hoped he was the only one to notice Whittemore's performance, but Soapy dispelled that wish, grunting with disgust. "Football player," he said scornfully. "Oh, brother!"

State chose to receive again, and the result was almost identical. A line thrust got two yards, a pass to Higgins was incomplete, and a sweep around Whittemore's end was spoiled by Western's right tackle, who brushed Whitty aside like the branch of a small tree.

Ace Gibbons got an opportunity to punt then and drove a good, high one down to the Western forty. Mike Brennan, charged with anger, sped down the field and brought the safety man to the ground with a jarring tackle. It set a good example but not good enough. Western started another march, concentrating on the left side of State's line, driving outside tackle and around Whittemore's end for consistent gains.

Mike Brennan and Ace Gibbons, playing in the linebacker positions of Ralston's defense, shifted to that side of the line. Then the Western quarterback sent a reverse around the other side of the line, and the ball carrier went all the way.

"Get ready," Soapy said, nudging Chip and Biggie. "Ralston's gonna put a football team in there in a minute."

Soapy was right. Ralston hadn't heard Soapy's words, but he substituted Chip for Lansing, Cohen for Morgan, Schwartz for Whittemore, Soapy for Clark, Finley for Gibbons, and Junior Roberts for Boots Cole right after the Western fullback sent the point-after kick spinning squarely between the uprights. So Western led 14-0, and it looked like a runaway.

Mike Brennan elected to receive once more, and State got its first break of the afternoon. The kick was short, straight to Finley on the twenty, and the husky bruiser bulled his way up the middle and across the mid-field stripe. State was in Western's territory for the first time.

Western took a time-out then. After the breather Chip brought the State bench to its feet by clever faking and then running to the right and pegging a forty-yard pass to Red Schwartz near the left sideline. Schwartz outran Western's defensive outside linebacker and dashed across the goal line for State's first score.

Buzz Burk held the ball for the extra-point attempt, and Chip booted a perfect placement to make the score Western 14, State 7.

Mike Brennan, grinning from ear to ear, came trotting up and cracked him on the back. "Atta baby, Chip," he said. "Nice going! They're receiving. You kick!"

It was the first time State's fighting captain had ever shown any friendliness, and Chip's chest tightened. "I'll kick it," he told himself, "clear into the woods!"

He nearly did it. Meeting the ball just right, he sent it end over end, over the goal line, and into the end zone. One of the Western backs downed the ball for the touchback, and the official carried it out to the twenty-yard line. It was Western's ball, first down and ten.

Western tried two unsuccessful short passes out into the flat. Now it was third down and ten yards to go. Chip was back in the free safety position of the defense, wholly unworried about helping cover for Red Schwartz, when Ralston sent Maxim in for Bill Carlson and Speed Morris for Junior Roberts. Checking the positions, he was struck by a sudden thought. With the exception of Red Schwartz for Philip Whittemore, the team Ralston had on the field now was the one he had selected as State's best the night after the guys had trounced the varsity. Not that Red Schwartz had to take a back seat to anyone—he had just proved that—but Chip felt Whittemore would be more valuable if protected from his own fears and given a little help.

Chip remembered something else. He had left the quarterback spot open. Well, he wasn't going to sell himself short. As he had said that morning at Camp All-America, time and Curly Ralston would take care of that decision.

Chip was startled out of his thoughts by the thump of foot meeting ball. One amazed glance and he turned and sprinted back upfield, chasing a ball bounding end over end along the ground and heading straight for State's end zone. Western's quarterback had caught him asleep and had called an audible at the line—a quick kick!

Behind him, Chip could hear the chug-chug of hard-running cleats. Someone was right on his tail and coming fast. Chip really turned on the speed then, mad at himself because he had been caught flat-footed. He knew the quick-kick protection a short punt formation afforded, but he had completely overlooked it while mooning about something that was none of his business: selecting State's starting lineup. "That won't happen again," he promised.

The ball had lost some of its speed now, and Chip was gaining. He edged to the right a bit and prepared to sweep the ball up on the dead run. He had to do it. He had to make up for going to sleep. If he fumbled this, it would be too bad. The guy behind him couldn't miss making the recovery.

"Turn right, Chip, turn right!"

Chip would have known that voice in a room with a thousand. Speed was chugging right behind him. He had sized up the situation and knew the lay of the land behind. Chip swerved left in a tight little circle, scooped up the ball without shortening his stride, and cut to the right. As soon as the ball was safely tucked under his arm, Chip glanced ahead and saw that Speed had figured it right. Only Western's right end was on that side of the field and close enough to give Chip immediate concern.

Speed demonstrated right then and there why he was varsity material. He headed for the big, rangy end at full speed and launched himself into a driving block. The speeding Westerner went down as if a giant had pulled the sod out from under him.

Chip was away! He sped up the left sideline, his long legs eating up the distance, picking up blockers along the way. Buzz Burk was first. The 170-pound speedster cut down Western's big center like straw from a broom. Then Fireball took out two of Western's big tackles with a wild, running block that spilled all three of them out-of-bounds and out of the play.

That did it! Chip could see touchdown daylight now with only Western's right halfback and the clever quarterback himself to worry about. Cohen easily took care of the quarterback, and Chip was on the Western fifteen with only the halfback between him and a touchdown. Behind him, he could hear pounding steps, and then he heard Soapy yell, "I'll take him, Chipper. Keep going!"

Chip was walking a tightrope along the sideline, straight for the apex of the angle toward which he and the Western player were speeding. But Western's final player never made the bone-shattering tackle he had planned. Soapy knocked the big back into and past Chip, but the back had no desire left to make the tackle. He and Soapy landed in a tangle of legs and arms and slid out-of-bounds. Chip slowed just an instant and then sped across the goal line.

CAUGHT ASLEEP!

Chip handed the ball to the official and took a deep breath. That had been close! Then a bunch of Statesmen ganged up and thumped him around. Mike Brennan and Tiny Tim McCarthy nearly knocked his helmet off, and Larry Higgins practically strangled him with a long arm around his neck. The Hilton A.C. got in their licks too. Chip was glad when they lined up for the extra point.

Chip was thinking how if he hadn't made that run, made up for going to sleep, he'd have been in trouble. He might have ruined his chances to win a starting berth. But that was football—one minute a hero, the next a "goat."

Burk held the ball again, and Chip kicked it into the woods. The ball split the uprights, and the score was tied: Western 14, State 14.

"Boot it again, Chip," Mike Brennan said, spitting on his hands and rubbing them together. "We got a team on this field now!" He looked to the left and to the right along the forty-yard line where his teammates waited and shouted, "Bet I make the tackle!"

Mike got the response he wanted. His challenge was loudly accepted. But Chip noticed Biggie Cohen and Fireball Finley wasted no time in yelling. They got set and watched him with alert eyes. Chip grinned. He didn't know Mike very well, but he knew Biggie and Fireball. Brennan was taking in a lot of territory by challenging those thirsty tacklers.

Chip kicked the ball into the end zone, and Western's left halfback made the mistake of gathering it in and starting upfield. Ralston used his kicker as safety after a kickoff, unless the kicker was a lineman too slow to stop a breakaway runner who might get loose on the kickoff. Chip and Tims Lansing were used as safeties. Chip remained back when he kicked off, and Tims Lansing took that assignment when Ace Gibbons or Mike Brennan kicked the ball.

After he had kicked, Chip slowed down to watch the fun but prepared to make sure of the tackle should the Western ball carrier break away. Brennan was speeding on a line for the runner, his body bent forward, broad back boring straight ahead, arms swinging. He ran through Western's wedge as if it wasn't there.

Biggie and Fireball flanked Mike, matching strides and heading for the runner as though he was a mortal enemy. "He hasn't got a chance," Chip whispered. "They'll smear him!"

But Chip was wrong. Mike, Biggie, and Fireball had the runner in a pocket, all right, but Soapy Smith beat all three of them to the target.

Soapy had yelled as loudly as anyone else in accepting Mike Brennan's challenge, but he hadn't neglected to get set for the dash. Soapy was slightly behind Fireball but closer to the sideline. The kick was a bit on that side, and Soapy had a straighter line to the ball carrier. The humorist was playing for keeps on this one and took off like a speeding arrow, flashing past Fireball at the last instant to nail the runner with a vicious flying tackle on the ten-yard line.

Biggie, Fireball, and Mike were moving so fast and were so intent on the tackle that they couldn't stop. They met with a crash, flew over the top of Soapy and the runner, and landed in a heap on the five-yard line. Soapy was up almost as soon as they landed, solicitously helping each to his feet and apologizing for his rudeness in depriving them of the great honor of grinding an enemy's nose in the dust.

"I'm really extremely sorry," he said piously. "The next time I'll hold back. Honest!"

CHAPTER 16

The Super Seven

WESTERN WAS now still as cocky and confident of running over State as it had been in the beginning of the game. But, as Captain Mike Brennan had proclaimed on the kickoff, "State has a team on this field now," and things were suddenly different. Western couldn't gain a foot. Brennan, Biggie, Silent Joe, Tiny Tim, Soapy, Schwartz, and Higgins were in Western's backfield almost as soon as the ball. Mike and Fireball almost came to blows in their desperate battle to make all the tackles. Speed began calling the line the "Super Seven," and in their vigor they almost tackled one another trying to get to the ball carrier.

On third and ten, Western's big fullback moved back into the end zone and booted a high punt to Chip on the home-team thirty-eight. Chip was surrounded by tacklers and signaled for a fair catch. Mike Brennan called time.

Rockwell, who had stood silently on the fifty-yard line during the entire scrimmage, now moved to

Ralston's side and spoke in a low voice. "Try Whittemore again, Curly. Try him with Hilton."

Ralston was surprised, but he didn't hesitate. He turned to the bench and bellowed: "Whittemore for Schwartz! Hustle, now!" He eyed Rockwell curiously. "Any special reason, Rock?"

Rockwell shook his head. "No, just a little experiment."

Judging by the results, Rockwell figured it was a good experiment. On the first play Chip faked a pass to Whittemore and kept going with the ball for a fifteen-yard gain. That put the ball on the home twenty-three, and Western called for a time-out. In the huddle, Chip moved over beside Whittemore. "You remember how you came off the trampoline this summer and swung around the upright?" he asked.

Whittemore nodded uncertainly, "Sure, Chip. Why?"

"Listen! On the second down, head straight for the right side of the goal post, pivot, and run for the left side. Got it? OK. I'll give you a hard, high pass right in front of the post. You'll have to jump for it!"

Chip ran a split buck with Fireball carrying the ball on the first down; Finley hit for four yards. On the next down Chip ran the takeoff play, faked a handoff to Fireball as he sped past, faked again to Speed cutting to the right, and dropped back in the passing pocket. There he cocked his arm and started a pass to Speed out in the right flat. At the last instant he pivoted and pegged a hard, high pass toward the left side of the goal post.

Whittemore had cut diagonally toward the right side of the goal post and was closely played by Western's strong safety. Three of his long running strides carried him to the right side before he turned and leaped in the air in front of the left side of the upright. It was timed perfectly, and Whittemore couldn't miss the catch. He pulled the ball in tight and fell in the end zone for the touchdown. With Speed holding, Chip again drove the ball between the uprights for the extra point, and State led 21-14.

Western was fighting mad, elected to receive, and ran Chip's goal-line kick to its own twenty-eight. Chip lined up beside Speed in the defensive huddle and asked him to trade positions again.

"Do you think it's all right?" Speed asked doubtfully. "You think Ralston—"

"You're better than I am back there," Chip interrupted. "Anyway, I want to get Biggie's goat."

Chip moved over to the defensive left halfback position when the huddle broke, jabbing Whittemore in the ribs on the way. "Dump the interference, Whitty," he said loudly. "I'll take the tackle!"

Biggie and Fireball looked at each other and laughed. "Seems I've heard that before," Biggie drawled.

"Yeah," Fireball added. "Sounds familiar. Some people never learn."

Rockwell was pacing the sideline behind Ralston, his sharp black eyes watching every move on the field. When Chip traded defensive spots with Speed Morris, Rock smiled whimsically and muttered something unintelligible. Ralston heard him but kept his eyes on the action on the field. "What did you say, Rock?"

"It can wait," Rockwell said quietly.

Western was a tough team, possessed a good running attack, and was dangerous in the air. And the Westerners were boiling. On the first play the big fullback went through the middle for a six-yard gain. The quarterback gambled on a short pass to his left end in the flat, and it clicked, chiefly because the receiver was six-three and caught the pass high above Buzz Burk's desperate leap. Buzz made the tackle, but the pass was good for six and a first down on the Western forty.

Western's field general sent his burly left halfback over Cohen's tackle on the first play, and Biggie and Fireball nearly tore him apart, dumping him on his back five yards behind the line of scrimmage. The big back got slowly to his feet and gave Biggie and Fireball a long look. Back in the huddle, he shook his head and informed his surprised quarterback that he could carry the ball himself if he wanted to try to gain through those two gorillas.

Speed batted down a long pass. Mike Brennan met the tough fullback right at the line of scrimmage for no gain, and Western was forced to kick. Brennan called for a 6-3-2 defense in the huddle, and Chip dropped back in the third line of defense with Speed. The punt was low and long, and it forced Chip and Speed back to State's fifteen-yard line. Chip started for the ball and then changed his mind. "Take it, Speed," he cried. "Follow me!" Chip led the way to the right, hoping Speed could get away. "He's got to," Chip muttered. "That will make it perfect."

Chip was moving, leading the way to the right sideline. He passed up the first tackler because the Westerner didn't slow down. Speed wouldn't have any trouble with him.

Speed was pounding along right behind Chip at the forty, then they were at midfield, and it was now or never because two Westerners were dead ahead, side by side. Chip ducked his head to get a reaction and then threw a cross-body block that mowed them both down. Speed sped past and Chip scrambled to his feet in time to see Western's left tackle force his teammate out-of-bounds on the home thirty. It was a beautiful runback, and Chip couldn't resist a shout of joy. Speed had come through.

Ralston sent in a new team then. The line was replaced by Curtis, Schwartz, Morgan, Carlson, Clark, Anderson, and Leopoulos. Tims Lansing, Boots Cole, Ace Gibbons, and Junior Roberts reported for the backfield.

Whittemore caught up with Chip and trotted off the field by his side. No words were spoken, but Chip knew Whitty was trying to express his feelings. Chip was happy. It had been a good day. His plans for Whitty were working out better than he had dreamed, and every member of the Valley Falls crew had proved to be *real* football player material. It had been a long step. He sighed contentedly and relaxed.

The next instant Chip was on his feet. "Oh, no!" he cried. But it was no use. Junior Roberts had fumbled on the very first play, and Western had recovered the ball. He dropped back on the bench only to leap up seconds later to repeat his cry of dismay. Western's left halfback had taken a direct handoff from his quarterback, faked off tackle, and then looked upfield to pass. He stabbed his right foot in the turf and fired a long pass down the far sideline.

Western's lanky left end never broke stride, stretched his arms high in the air, and gathered in the ball. It was as disastrously sudden and easy as one-two-three. The big player raced all the way, leaving Junior Roberts and Tims Lansing far behind. The Western fullback kicked the extra point, and it was a new ball game. The score was Western 21, State 21.

Curly Ralston must have figured it was a good time to quit, and the Western coach must have felt the same way. At any rate, they held a short consultation at midfield and then sent the players to the showers.

TEN SECONDS TO PLAY!

The Westerners proved to be great guys off the field, and by tacit agreement, it seemed, all football talk was taboo during dinner. The players of both squads said good-bye after the meal with sincere wishes for successful seasons, especially since they weren't scheduled to play each other. Soapy got in the last word from the window of his bus. "See you in the Rose Bowl," he yelled. "I hope, I hope!"

It was after midnight when they reached Camp Sundown. The players stumbled sleepily out of the bus, glad to be home and eager to hit their bunks. No one wanted to think about rising at seven o'clock in the morning.

Ralston startled most of them out of their lethargy, and they yelped their appreciation when he announced, "Breakfast at nine! Practice at four o'clock tomorrow afternoon."

Soapy couldn't understand it. "Poor guy," he said sympathetically. "He must be sick. I hope, I hope!"

Ralston wasn't sick. He was full of pep and wide awake. "Come on, you guys," he said briskly, grabbing Rockwell and Nelson each by an arm and hurrying them along. "We'll get us a pot of coffee and have a little skull practice all our own."

"But it's nearly one o'clock," Nelson protested. "Can't it wait until morning?"

"No!" Ralston said briskly. "Too important!"

"OK," Nelson agreed, "but there ought to be a law."

Ralston got the coffee going and then joined his coaches at the kitchen table. "Well," he asked, "what do you think now?"

"Sophs looked good," Nelson said firmly. "Hilton and Finley and Cohen—" He shook his head and grinned wryly. "Don't see how you can keep them off. Right, Rock?"

Rockwell shrugged, "They looked good to me."

"And Whittemore?" Ralston suggested, shifting his glance searchingly from Rockwell to Nelson and back to Rockwell.

Neither coach answered, and Ralston repeated the question. "Well, what about Whittemore? Rock, you had something in mind this afternoon when you asked me to try him with Hilton. What was it?"

"I don't know whether I can explain it or not," Rockwell said thoughtfully, "but for some reason, he looks only halfway like a football player when he's in there with Lansing."

"That's hard to figure," Ralston said slowly. "He played high school ball with Lansing. They ought to know each other's every move. I don't get it."

"I think the guy's overrated," Nelson said shortly.

"That isn't what you told me a year ago," Ralston reminded him. "Remember?"

"I remember, all right. Maybe the competition—" The coffee was ready by this time, and Ralston served. They sat in silence for a few seconds, and then Nelson changed the subject. "I wish some of the alumni could have seen the scrimmage this afternoon. It might have changed their minds about a few things."

"Meaning what?" Ralston demanded.

"Meaning they'd have seen some real stars in action, real football players! A few players besides Lansing, Gibbons, Cole, Clark, Morgan, and Carlson," Nelson said pointedly.

"You really feel that way, Nik?" Ralston asked, eyeing his young assistant steadily.

"Yes, Coach, I do!" Nelson said firmly.

"And you, Rock?" Ralston asked.

"You're the boss, Curly," Rockwell said slowly. "You'll have to make the decision."

Ralston sighed deeply. "I already have," he said softly.

Rockwell and Nelson waited expectantly for him to continue.

"Once in a long time, once in a blue moon," Ralston continued thoughtfully, "a player comes along with the spark of greatness that can mean the difference between a mediocre team and a great one. This spark of greatness or spirit or soul or genius—call it what you wish—is a combination of wisdom, leadership, intuition, loyalty, and unwavering courage.

"Sometimes this spark is hidden behind a personality that conceals its presence; it's a lucky coach who penetrates the barrier."

There was just the trace of a smile of affection on his lips and around his eyes when Ralston paused and looked at Rockwell. Then it disappeared. "Rock, you've added greatly to your stature in my eyes during the past three weeks. You've known all along it would be a tragic mistake to keep a certain player on the sidelines. But, despite your personal interest and friendship for the player, you never once tried to bring any pressure to bear on his behalf. I like that, like it a lot.

"But regardless of likes and dislikes, gentlemen— and that goes for the alumni and anyone else, Nik—we're starting as of right now to break up a team that every football fan in the state thinks is invincible. We're going to break it up and build a far greater one, a team that may prove to be one of the greatest in State football history—chiefly because of the spark of greatness, leadership, and team spirit of its quarterback, Chip Hilton!"

CHAPTER 17

The Breakup Game

TIMS LANSING was an intelligent college senior who had a good mind and a lot of fine ambitions. He loved football for what it was, a contact game that gave an athlete a chance to prove he was all man, and he could take it when the going got tough as well as dish it out when everything was rosy. Tims had started every game for State the previous year and had set his heart on finishing his football career in a blaze of glory. He had recognized Chip as a dangerous contender for his job and had gone all out in the workouts and scrimmages in an attempt to prove he was the better player.

All the time Curly Ralston was talking to Rockwell and Nelson, and long after they had gone to sleep, Tims remained awake, facing the realization that Chip Hilton was the better football player. It was hard to take.

The next morning Lansing and Whittemore took a long walk. Tims was two years older than Whitty, but they had been hometown friends even though Tims had been a senior in high school when Whitty was a junior. Knowing how much Tims loved football, Whitty was shocked beyond words by Lansing's abrupt revelation.

"I lost a job yesterday," Tims said calmly. "Hilton beat me out for the starting quarterback spot."

"What? How?"

"Hilton's a better player," Tims continued, "a better runner, passer, and kicker. Anyone who saw him yesterday against Western and stopped to think about it realizes it as well as I do. I'm not in his league."

"You mean that?" Whittemore said, astonished. "You think Ralston will make him a starter? He's only a sophomore!"

"That doesn't make any difference, Whitty. You've heard Ralston say a dozen times that the best man gets the job. Well, Hilton's the best man."

Whittemore learned a great deal about sportsmanship and football during that walk. And he learned a lot about Tims Lansing. "What are you going to do?" he asked.

Tims grinned. "Exactly what I'm supposed to do. I'm going to block the daylights out of him and tackle him and rough him up every time I get a chance, so he'll be even better than he is now, and then when Saturday rolls around and I'm sitting on the bench, I'm going to pull for him as if he were my own brother."

"You mean you're not going to quit?"

"Quit?" Tims repeated incredulously. "Are you crazy? Football players never quit! Now let's talk about you."

Lansing didn't pull any punches. He told Whittemore the regulars thought he was a show-off and couldn't understand why he didn't put out during the tackling and blocking drills. "You're one of my best friends,

Whitty, but you don't seem to understand that football is a team game. You're expected to sacrifice for your teammates just as they do for you. You've got to do your part when it comes to tackling and blocking and taking the lumps. I've watched you from the first day of practice, and you slack off when it's time for the rough stuff. The rest of the guys have been watching you too. And they don't like it!

"Ralston needs ends, big ones like you. I guess that's the reason the coaching staff has let you get away with it. C'mon, Whitty. We're from the same town, and they're expecting us to be good. What do you say? Let's show them we're team players, OK?"

"OK, Tims," Whittemore said resolutely. "I will."

Peculiarly, Whittemore seemed to be on everyone's mind in camp that morning. Chip was loosening up on the basketball court, and between shots he was thinking two weeks ahead to the opening of school when he would have a chance to talk to Dr. Edna Smith about Whittemore's problem. Maybe he could get Whitty to come along.

The other members of the Hilton A.C., along with Fireball Finley, were trying to cheer up Red Schwartz. Red was down, all upset because he was the only member of the Valley Falls contingent who seemed doomed to sit the bench.

"I wouldn't mind sitting the bench behind a real player," he griped, "but this Whittemore can't do anything but catch passes. He won't block or even try to make any kind of a tackle except one of those half-speed deals that doesn't mean anything. He even seems to have Chip fooled." Red turned appealingly to his listeners. "Am I wrong or not?"

"Not as far as I'm concerned," Soapy growled. "The guy's riding Chip's shirttails just because they worked together at that camp."

"I can't understand why Chip sticks up for him," Morris said in disgust. "Chip's always telling him something in the huddle and patting him on the back and making a fuss every time he catches a pass."

"I don't know about that," Cohen drawled. "We're doing a lot of talking without knowing the facts. Let's ask Chip. He's up on the basketball court. C'mon!"

It was delicate. When the guys got up to the court and greeted Chip, no one wanted to make the break. Chip helped when he stopped shooting and challenged them to a game of Twenty-One. "C'mon," he said, "loosen up! Soapy, Biggie, and I will take on you three. C'mon, Speed. How about it, Red?"

"Not me," Red said bitterly. "I came to this camp to try to play football. Maybe I ought to forget football and take up basketball at that."

"What are you talking about?" Chip demanded. "You're doing as well as anybody else."

"Not quite, Chip," Biggie said, choosing his words carefully. "That's why we came up here to see you. We wanted to talk to you about Red and, well, Whittemore."

"What's Red got to do with Whittemore?"

It was a difficult conversation for all of them. Chip was bound by his promise to Whittemore, and Red was uncomfortably self-conscious. "I'm not jealous of the guy, Chip," he said. "Honest! If he can beat me out, more power to him. But he ought to have to fight for the job, not get it handed to him on a silver platter."

Chip nodded. "You're right, Red. But that's Ralston's problem," he said gently, "not mine. I'm trying to help Whittemore for an entirely different reason than football. All of you, and particularly you, Red, will just have to believe me when I say that Whittemore desperately needs my help. Unfortunately, I can't tell you the whole story. I know it's a lot to ask but—"

"That's good enough for me, Chip," Red said impulsively. "Let's forget it. I'm a chump."

Things moved fast after Ralston revised his varsity depth chart. The displaced veterans didn't like it, but no one would have known it by their attitudes. Troubles Morgan, Wally Curtis, Dex Clark, Bill Carlson, Boots Cole, and Buzz Burk proved to be good sportsmen first and good football players second. They didn't quit hustling and made it clear to Chip, Soapy, Biggie, Fireball, Speed, and Silent Joe Maxim that the sophomores couldn't let down and still expect to start against Tech on Saturday, October 2, at University Stadium.

Philip Whittemore had a rough time. Despite the efforts of Tims Lansing, the veterans poured it on him at every opportunity. Fireball and the Valley Falls guys didn't ride him, but they didn't go out of their way to give him any help either.

Whittemore's spirits dropped lower and lower every day. He tried to cover it up, but he couldn't hide his heavy heart from his true friend. Chip experienced the frustration a friend always feels when someone desperately needs his help, and he can't do anything about it.

The last week of camp was the toughest. It had been a long, tough training period without a letup except for Sundays. The boys didn't feel like doing anything that day except going to church and then heading for their bunks to rest their tired and bruised muscles.

Ralston really poured it on Wednesday afternoon. And, for the first time, the members of the coaching staff began to show the strain of the long training session.

Chip knew sooner or later one of the coaches would get on Whittemore. Unfortunately, Nik Nelson was working with the ends on special group work and caught Whittemore going halfheartedly through the motions on a blocking assignment.

Nelson couldn't take it. He shocked the big end and everyone on the field when his voice and temper got out of control. It was the first time any player had been dressed down publicly, and Nik went all the way, his contempt for Whittemore's kind of football out in the open at last.

Chip wanted to stop him, and tell Nelson, Ralston, Rockwell, and every player on the field that Whittemore couldn't help it, that it was something entirely beyond his control. It took all his will power to hold back the flood of words that leaped to his lips. As soon as practice was over, he hurried to Whittemore's side. Whittemore was completely broken. His face was deathly white, and his eyes were full of the terrible hurt that public humiliation can bring to any athlete at any age.

"That's the end, Chip. I can't stand any more."

"It wasn't nice, Whitty. Nelson didn't mean all that. He's as tired as you are and I am, and everyone else is."

"He was right, Chip. That's what hurts. I haven't got any business playing football. I don't belong."

"That's not true! You do belong. You are a good football player. And you've got some good friends who know you are—Tims Lansing, the Dodds, and me! Look, Whitty, we started out to whip this thing together. We knew it wasn't going to be easy. I'm not quitting, and I'm not going to let you quit either. There's only three more days to go. After that, it will be easy. We'll be in school, the games will be coming up, and after we get a couple under our belts, this thing will be whipped. I know it!"

THE BREAKUP GAME

Chip went to bed that night afraid Whittemore would be gone in the morning. But Whitty was there the next morning, and he stuck it out until Saturday.

The big day came at last, and Camp Sundown started to buzz with action at the crack of dawn. Cars loaded with alumni football enthusiasts were pouring in from all over the state. The annual "breakup" scrimmage game always attracted a large crowd, but a special magnet attracted the fans this day.

The news filtering out of Camp Sundown for the past week had startled the fans, and they wanted to be present at the breakup scrimmage to see for themselves. Each fan discussed the startling situation as if he alone knew the inside story.

"Six sophomores! Three of them in the backfield!"

"Never heard anything like it! Breaking up a veteran team."

"I can't see a bunch of kids playing that schedule."

"They better be awful good. First game's only a week away."

"What if they are good? They're still kids. No experience."

"The *Herald* ran a whole column about it."

"That was Bill Bell's story. He said they were sensational. I'll reserve judgment until Saturday. Tech's tough!"

"Bell's an old man. Still writing noseguard football."

"I don't know much about those other sophomores, but I saw Hilton last year. I never saw a better football player."

"Lots of freshman big shots turn out to be sophomore busts."

"Ralston's a good coach. He knows what he's doing!"

By two o'clock, there wasn't an empty parking spot within half a mile of Camp Sundown. The low bleachers on each side of the field were jammed, and every foot of space around the white boundary lines was occupied by standing fans.

One of the managers photocopied a simple program listing the starting teams. The back listed the complete varsity roster alphabetically. A few of these fluttered on the ground, and others rested in pockets for future reference, but most of them were clutched in hands so the new stars could be identified as they appeared.

"Where are their names on the uniforms?" someone asked loudly.

"Coaching staff doesn't believe in names on player uniforms. The name on the front is what counts!"

"Here they come! Which one of those guys is Hilton?"

"The big guy on the end must be Whittemore. Bell says he's great!"

"Program says he's six-four and weighs 210. That's him, all right."

TEAM A

L.E.	Whittemore	21	6-4	210	Jr.
L.T.	Cohen	19	6-4	240	Soph.
L.G.	McCarthy	22	5-11	245	Sr.
C.	Brennan	22	6-0	205	Jr.
R.G.	Smith	19	6-0	200	Soph.
R.T.	Maxim	19	6-2	195	Soph.
R.E.	Higgins	22	6-5	180	Sr.
Q.B.	Hilton	19	6-4	185	Soph.
L.H.	Morris	19	5-11	170	Soph.
F.B.	Finley	19	6-0	210	Soph.
R.H.	Gibbons	21	6-0	200	Jr.

THE BREAKUP GAME

TEAM B

L.E.	Curtis	21	6-3	198	Sr.
L.T.	Morgan	23	6-4	190	Sr.
L.G.	Anderson	18	5-9	185	Soph.
C.	Leopoulos	19	6-2	190	Soph.
R.G.	Clark	23	5-8	180	Sr.
R.T.	Carlson	24	6-2	188	Sr.
R.E.	Schwartz	19	5-11	175	Soph.
Q.B.	Lansing	22	6-1	180	Sr.
L.H.	Cole	23	5-11	165	Sr.
F.B.	Roberts	19	6-3	230	Soph.
R.H.	Burk	23	5-9	170	Sr.

"You realize there are only two seniors on the starting offensive team?"

"Hey! Ace Gibbons has been moved from fullback to right half."

"That guy Finley must be pretty good if he beat Gibbons out of the fullback job."

"They say this guy Hilton kicks the ball into the end zone just like a pro."

Chip did kick the ball into the end zone and out-of-bounds, and that start was a tip-off on how the breakup game was to go. Team A was too big, too fast, and had too many young guns. Chip could do nothing wrong; he handled the ball like a magician, fooling the spectators and the opposition time after time with his sleight of hand. He ran the ball for good gains, and his kicking was superb. Playing defensive left halfback, he was able to help Whittemore on the defense, and his instructions in the huddle resulted in Whittemore making several sensational catches. Team A scored almost at will and pinned Team B inside its own fifty all afternoon. The breakup game ended with the score: Team A 35, Team B 0.

TEN SECONDS TO PLAY!

So the breakup game became history, the training season was over, the members of the Hilton A. C. all made the State University varsity squad, and a certain prophesy was coming true.

The Valley Falls stars had visited State three years earlier to get a look at the college of their choice, and Soapy Smith had proclaimed, "We'll be taking over up here in a couple of years!"

CHAPTER 18

End on the Run

MITZI SAVRILL was at the cashier's desk counting change. Soapy Smith, Fireball Finley, and Philip Whittemore were behind the counter serving pizza, hamburgers, Cokes, and ice-cream treats, and Chip Hilton was taking inventory in the storeroom. It was the first day of classes, and anyone who dropped in at Grayson's for an ice-cream cone or a quick snack might have remembered the employees were all doing about the same thing last June—with the exception of the new guy with the football shoulders, who didn't seem to know much about the food service business.

Otherwise, things were just about the same. Chip, Soapy, Biggie, Speed, and Red were living in Jefferson Hall again. Pete Randolph, the resident assistant, had given them the same old rooms. Pete, as usual, had jokingly grumbled and griped when the new resident moved in. Yet the reception wasn't as bad as it might have been, because Philip Whittemore was a friend of Jeff's dorm president, and Pete liked Chip Hilton.

Monday had been the busiest day in Chip's life. He had recommended Whittemore to George Grayson for a job, and Whitty had started that night. Chip had gotten all set with his class schedule, met his professors, reported for football practice, presided at the first meeting of Jeff's executive council, and visited with Dr. Smith, one of State's most popular psychology professors.

Dr. Smith had been quite surprised by the interest State's newest sports hero evidenced in psychology case studies, but she was also a bit flattered. Chip got a first-class analysis of the case problem that had "bothered him all summer."

Chip learned that Whittemore, the subject in the case study, was probably attempting "flight from memory," which might be cured if he could be encouraged to face the problem. "The subject is a victim of repression and tends to exclude from consciousness unpleasant ideas or action," Dr. Smith said.

"Now, Chip," Smith summarized, "if your friend could be encouraged to face the block and analyze it and remove it from his mind, normal action would result. This type of person needs the help of someone who is strong, someone he can lean on in times of stress. This someone must be aggressive where the friend is concerned and force him to action. Confusing?"

Chip nodded. It was confusing, but he decided to risk one more question. "Would this person have to be shocked out of his condition?"

Smith shook her head, "No, of course not. This case isn't serious at all. The subject—your friend—must be forced in some way to analyze the problem and encouraged to take steps to overcome the block. That's where a friend or someone he trusts comes in. This person must keep after him and impress upon him the absolute necessity of forcing the block out of his mind when action is necessary."

Chip followed Smith's information. He kept after Whittemore at Jeff, on the campus, at football practice, and in the evenings at Grayson's.

Everything seemed to be under control. Then Curly Ralston pulled a fast one! He surprised everyone by holding a secret scrimmage Tuesday afternoon against Western—a return practice game—and this one was for keeps! The season for Western and State opened just four days later, and each squad went all out.

Ralston started his revamped offensive lineup, and it was touch and go. State scored first, receiving the kickoff and marching right down the field to score. Chip ran the team superbly, mixing his line and flank attack with sure, short passes. It was beautiful quarterbacking.

Both coaches substituted freely, and Western tied the score later in the period. In the abbreviated last quarter, with the score tied 14-14 and a scant twenty seconds to go, State had the ball at midfield, fourth down and ten to go. Chip hurried the Statesmen into a huddle, calling for a long pass and calling Whittemore's number with the alternate being Speed Morris. But Chip was rushed, couldn't get the pass away, and was forced to run. And, as often happens when opponents drop back to cover receivers, Chip got clear away.

Running brilliantly, Chip eluded several desperate tacklers and had a clear path to the goal except for the strong safety, who was covering Whittemore. This player left Whittemore and advanced warily to stop Chip's touchdown run. He was beautifully set up for Whittemore, and a simple block would have done the trick. But Whittemore made only a futile, halfhearted attempt, sprawling awkwardly on the ground, and the Western halfback dropped Chip on the fifteen-yard line, ending the game. That scrimmage game didn't count in the records, but it meant a lot to State's new varsity.

State's locker room was quiet after the game. Too quiet. Whittemore couldn't avoid the disgusted glances of his teammates, and the big player dressed without a word and hurried out of the room. Chip couldn't do much about it right then. It wasn't the time or the place.

That evening Whittemore showed up for his job at Grayson's, but he was completely dejected. Chip tried to cheer him up and even Soapy chimed in. When Soapy took his break, Chip relieved him at the counter and redoubled his efforts.

Shortly after Soapy left, two pretty students, trim enough to afford the luxury, ordered Soapy's special banana splits. Chip served them and, without intending to do so, caught snippets of their conversation.

"That was the summer my family rented a cottage at Pleasant Harbor."

"That's a nice name for a town."

"Pleasant Harbor" shocked Chip! He whirled around to look at the speaker. She was deeply absorbed in her story.

"It was nice until the day Mom and Dad went to New York and left me alone at the cottage. I thought I had told you about it. It was horrible."

"What happened?"

Chip became so absorbed in the story that he neglected several customers. They coughed impatiently, and he hurried to serve them, his heart beating with excitement. Pleasant Harbor! What a break! This was it!

END ON THE RUN

He turned back to the two girls. But they had disappeared! Hustling around the end of the counter, he dashed out to the street, ice-cream dipper still clutched in his hand, and looked wildly about. The girls were not in sight. He rushed to the corner and back again and then across the street, where two young freshman students were looking in a shop window. He edged up and looked closely at their faces.

The nearest girl turned quickly and caught his glance. Chip's appearance evidently amused her. "Oh, one of the college guys," she said, giggling.

The other girl nodded delightedly, enjoying Chip's embarrassment. "Sure he is! He must be getting initiated in one of those fraternities!"

Chip turned and fled back to the drugstore, looking frantically to the left and to the right. "How could they disappear so quickly?" he muttered. "I've got to find them!" He hurried to the cashier's desk to meet Mitzi's puzzled violet-blue eyes.

"What's gotten into you, Chip?" Mitzi began.

"Did you see those two girls? The two who ordered Soapy's special banana splits?"

"Of course, Chip. Anything wrong?"

"No! Yes! Something important!" Chip looked through the window at the passing faces. Then an expression of hope flashed back to his eyes. "Do you know them?"

Mitzi flashed her most dazzling smile. "No, Chip, I don't. All I remember about them is that they were rather attractive and their check amounted to $ 4.90 plus tax. Which one's the lucky one?"

Chip muttered something under his breath and rushed back to the storeroom. He grabbed a startled Soapy Smith by the arm, "I'll be right back! Help Whitty at the counter."

TEN SECONDS TO PLAY!

Chip didn't even look at Mitzi when he hurried out of the store, and this was so unlike Chip that Mitzi immediately made one of her rare mistakes. She gave the next customer change for a twenty-dollar bill instead of change for the rumpled ten the customer had given her.

"I gave you a ten-dollar bill," the man said, smiling and pushing the money back. "That young man got you upset?"

Chip was more than upset. He patrolled Tenth Street for an hour, peering furtively at the face of every girl he met. But he had no luck and returned dejectedly to Grayson's. In the storeroom he dropped wearily into the chair by the desk. Soapy followed and looked at him anxiously. "You sick?" he asked.

"I guess you could call it that," Chip answered disconsolately.

Soapy's face grew serious. "What's wrong?"

"Well, a couple of girls were sitting at the counter a while ago, and they were talking about something that means a lot to me. Well, to make a long story short, while I was waiting on someone else, they left. I've been looking for them ever since."

"What did they look like?"

"One was tall and slim and had a fair complexion. I think her hair was sort of a dark brown, and she was wearing it down around her shoulders. The other was a blonde and short. She has a short nose, and I guess you'd call it a peaches-and-cream complexion. I think she had brown eyes, but she was wearing glasses, and I don't know for sure."

"That's Cuddles!" Soapy interrupted excitedly. "Gotta be! You know why? 'Cause she's like Mitzi, only different. Another thing! They order splits? I thought so! Sure, I know them! The tall girl is Elizabeth Baker. Her dad's on the faculty. They're old, regular customers. I met them last year. Love banana splits. Come in here every night. Why, I even know Cuddles's telephone number. Now what do you want ol' Soapy to do?"

"Get us a double date. Tonight, tomorrow night, right away!"

"You kidding? You feel all right? Are you the *real* Chip Hilton?"

Chip assured Soapy he was all right, but it took Soapy Smith all evening to get over the shock. Soapy still couldn't believe Chip had asked him to set up a date for him. But Soapy arranged the date for the following evening.

"Now all you have to do," he told Chip dubiously, "is raise movie money and get us the night off—our first week back on the job after being away for three months."

Wednesday's practice was a real ordeal for Whittemore. Some of the veterans sneered openly at him, and a few others muttered remarks. Chip was desperately worried that Whittemore might quit again when Coach Ralston demoted the big receiver to the second team. Whittemore all but died right there when Red took his place. He brightened up a bit when Chip slapped him on the back, but when Chip passed Grayson's on the way to meet the girls, he made sure that Whittemore was at work.

Not surprisingly, Chip had a nice time. Elizabeth Baker proved to be a lot of fun and a member of Chip's class. They went to a movie and later to the Sweet Shop for two Cokes and two banana splits. Both girls agreed they weren't as good as Soapy's specials. Soapy made sure they gave Grayson's a wide detour. Mitzi Savrill was the unattainable love of his life.

The only flaw in the evening, as far as Soapy was concerned, was Chip's absorption in Elizabeth's story of a frightening, near-drowning experience at a seashore resort named Pleasant Harbor. Soapy interrupted several times to talk about football and to tell the girls about the article and photo of Chip in the morning paper, but Chip always turned the conversation back to Elizabeth's long-ago vacation episode. The girls were thrilled to be in the company of two of State's new football stars, and Elizabeth asked them to come to dinner at her home Friday evening.

"We couldn't make it Friday," Soapy explained. "You see, that's the night before the first game, and we've got to look at films of last year's game and hit the rack by eleven o'clock."

Elizabeth settled for seven o'clock the following evening. "I want you to meet my parents," she said proudly.

Soapy couldn't keep up with Chip on the way to Jeff. Chip was thrilled and could hardly keep from running. It was true! That was the same girl, and it was the story of Whittemore's Pleasant Harbor experience right down to the very last detail! He had the solution to all of Whittemore's problems right in the palm of his hand! Whittemore would be home from work now, and was he in for a surprise!

"See you in a few minutes," Chip said jubilantly, thumping Soapy in the ribs, then taking the steps leading to Jeff's third floor three at a time. "I've got to see Whittemore."

He pounded on the door and waited expectantly. But there was no answer; he cautiously opened the door. The room was empty, but everything was in confusion: bureau drawers were empty and pulled out, and clothes hangers, papers, and discarded articles of clothing covered the floor.

END ON THE RUN

Chip dashed down the stairs, back to Pete Randolph's room on the first floor, and pounded on the door. Inside, he could hear Randolph muttering and griping.

Then the door was flung open. "Well, what do you want now, freshman?" Randolph demanded impatiently. Then, seeing it was Chip, his manner changed. "What's up, Chip?"

"Whittemore, Pete. Have you seen him?"

"Yes. I saw him just before he left, said he's going home. Mentioned something about the midnight bus. He seemed pretty low about something."

Chip had heard enough. He turned and dashed out the front door. "Ten minutes," he breathed. "Got to hurry! If I can only get a cab!" Then he was struck with another thought. *What if someone sees me? Well, can't help it! This is an emergency!*

CHAPTER 19

Elizabeth's Story

UNIVERSITY TAXI drivers are used to the "I'm in a hurry" rides of university students, and Chip's driver got him to the bus station with three minutes to spare. Chip thrust some bills in the driver's hand and dashed for the waiting room. There were only a few people in the terminal, and Chip was relieved to see Whittemore was one of them. He was just picking up his backpack when Chip ran up, tore it out of his hand, and dropped it on the floor with a bang.

"Where do you think you're going?" Chip demanded, grabbing Whittemore by the arm. "You can't do this to me! Not after I've stood up for you, believed in you, nearly lost my friends for you. I ought to give you the thumping of your life right here! Right in the middle of this waiting room even if I get arrested! You can't walk out on me now!"

"I wouldn't walk out on you, Chip. Honest. I—"

"You're right you wouldn't! Now you listen to me! You're going back to Jeff, and you're going to listen to what I have to say. You hear? It's the greatest thing that ever happened! I've got all the proof. Every bit of it! You don't have to worry another day as long as you live about what happened at Pleasant Harbor. Do you hear what I'm saying? All these years you've been worrying and running for nothing. You hear me? *It isn't true! It never happened—at least not the way you think it did!*"

"No, Chip, you're wrong," Whittemore said. "It's got to be true! I was there. It was my fault."

"It wasn't anyone's fault because it *didn't* happen! Are you deaf now too? Listen to me. It never happened! Nothing happened. And I've got all the proof. C'mon. We're going back to Jeff."

"But I've got my ticket—"

"Give it to me!"

Whittemore reluctantly handed the ticket over, and Chip grabbed it and jammed it down in his jacket pocket. "There," he said. "That takes care of that! You're never going to need that ticket! I'll cash it in for you next week! C'mon now. You're going with me!"

Chip half led Whittemore to the cab, and soon they were back at Jeff in Whittemore's room. Then Chip whipped out a pencil and a piece of paper and handed them to the bewildered athlete. "Now you write down, word for word, exactly what you told me at camp the night you walked back from Dalesburg. Everything that happened at Pleasant Harbor. Don't leave out a single word!"

Whittemore took the paper and looked at Chip, "This won't do any good, Chip. I—"

"Never mind, write it! No one is going to see it except you and me. But I want you to write down exactly what happened at Pleasant Harbor, so you can compare it word for word with the proof I'm going to show you tomorrow night. Proof that it's not true and proof that you can't deny to save your life."

Whittemore was bewildered and unnerved, but Chip was implacable. He stood in the middle of the room and didn't move until Whittemore finished writing the difficult note. Chip read it slowly and then folded it carefully and placed it in his pocket.

"You'll get this back tomorrow night, Whitty," he said kindly. "And I promise, not a soul will ever see it. Word of honor! But when I do give it back, all your troubles will be over."

"All right, Chip," Whittemore said. "That's fair enough. I haven't anything to lose, but I know you're wasting your time."

Soapy Smith studied hard, worked hard, played hard, and trained faithfully. Soapy never cheated on Coach Ralston's training rules, and Chip wanted him to get his well-deserved rest. So he undressed in the dark and got into bed as quietly as possible. The bond of friendship between Chip and Soapy and all of the members of the Hilton A.C. was built on a strong foundation. They all believed in helping one another and their friends.

"That you, Chip?"

"Yes, Soapy. I thought you were asleep."

"Can't sleep, Chip. I've been lying here thinking about Saturday. Just think, we're starting on the varsity Saturday against Tech. It seems almost like a dream."

There was a brief silence. Then, true to form, Soapy changed the subject, skipping abruptly to something bugging him. "Chip, what's with this date with Elizabeth Baker? I can't figure it out. Has this got something to do with Whittemore?"

Chip pondered a moment and then made his decision. "Yes, Soapy, it has. You would make a good lawyer. But that's all I can tell you. Do you mind?"

"Mind? Me? Of course not, Chipper. But how are we both going to get off from work tomorrow night?"

Chip smiled into the darkness. That was Soapy, all right, direct and on target. "We're not, Soapy. That is, if you don't care too much. Would it be all right if I took Whitty with me tomorrow—I mean, tonight? Do you think Cuddles would mind?"

"Cuddles? That's a laugh! Cuddles is a good friend. That's all, Chipper. There's only one true love in my life, and she's delightful, delicious, and delovely! Every time I think of those big violet-blue eyes and that smile, I—"

Chip laughed. "I know, Soapy, I know," he interrupted. "Mitzi's wonderful, out of this world, and she won't give you a second look! Right?"

Soapy grunted, "Humph! Wait and see! She's just trying to hold herself back."

Whittemore didn't show up for practice that afternoon, but he was waiting for Chip outside Grayson's at 6:30. Chip could see that Whitty was nervous, so Chip made sure he didn't talk too much about the evening and joked, "Whitty, why are you so stressed? Haven't you been on a date before?"

Then, more seriously, Chip added, "I think you'll remember this dinner as long as you live, Whitty. Remember, these people don't know anything about you. Don't know your name, where you are from, or why you're here. OK?"

Elizabeth Baker met them at the door and showed no surprise when Chip introduced Whitty and explained that Soapy had to work. She led them to the living room where her parents and Cuddles were waiting and made the introductions. Dr. Baker smiled and got to his feet when they entered, shaking their hands cordially.

Dinner was delicious; *Soapy would have enjoyed the desserts,* Chip thought. Afterward, they returned to the living room, and Dr. and Mrs. Baker guided the conversation to topics that might interest their guests. Chip was growing impatient to switch the conversation to Elizabeth's seashore experience. He got his chance when the talk turned to sports, and he immediately took advantage of it.

"Whitty's a wonderful diver," he said. "Maybe good enough for the Olympic team." It was a touchy subject for Whittemore, Chip knew, but he had no alternative.

Cuddles saved the day. "You ought to see Elizabeth swim," she volunteered.

Chip could have kissed her. And for Chip, that was quite a concession.

"She's pretty good," Professor Baker agreed proudly. "Elizabeth had a good reason for developing her swimming ability. Tell them about it, Beth."

Elizabeth protested, smiling and shaking her head. "Chip has heard all about that, Dad," she said self-consciously. "He wouldn't want to hear that all over again."

"You're wrong," Chip said quickly. "*Please* tell us about it. I know Whitty would like to hear it. Right, Whitty?"

Whittemore's face paled, and his embarrassment was obvious. But he managed to nod his head and mumble that he'd be delighted.

"All right," Elizabeth said reluctantly. Then she told about the time her family had rented a cottage at Pleasant Harbor for the summer. One day, her parents had driven to New York City, leaving her with specific instructions not to go into the ocean until they returned.

ELIZABETH'S STORY

The stretch of beach near their cottage was not used for swimming, and no lifeguard was stationed there. Elizabeth spent some time cleaning up the cottage and reading a book, but then she put on her bathing suit and walked down to the beach to work on her tan.

"It was early," Elizabeth said wistfully, "and the sun was dancing over the waves. The water was beautiful, and the breakers were rushing in to shore so majestically that I couldn't resist the temptation."

She paused and glanced contritely at her parents before continuing, "Anyway, I plunged in and started swimming. There wasn't a soul on the beach except a boy about my own age who was swimming some distance away. I guess I was just carried away by the recklessness of it."

"Pandora's box," Professor Baker said gently.

"The breakers were so powerful and yet so gentle when they hurled me back to the shore that I became bold and began to dive through and under them. Then—"

Elizabeth paused and shook her head ruefully, "Then I was caught in an undertow that was too strong for me, and it began to carry me out to sea. I swam as hard as I could, but it was no use. I was losing steadily, and the shore was getting farther away. I panicked and began screaming to the boy who was swimming some distance away. But he didn't hear me, and I was soon too far away for my voice to reach him. It was useless to fight the current, and I nearly gave up. Then I began to think of Mom and Dad, and I made up my mind to keep fighting as long as possible.

"Just when I was about exhausted, I saw a man fishing in a boat a little farther out. I shouted with my little remaining strength, and well, that's about all there is to it. The man heard me, pulled me in the boat, bundled me up in his coat, and took me in to shore farther down the beach. The beach patrol asked me a lot of questions, and when my parents got home, I caught it good—got grounded too. But I made up my mind right then that I would keep practicing until I was a strong swimmer, not a weak one."

Whittemore hadn't moved. Chip didn't dare glance at him to see his reaction, but he was determined to clinch it once and for all. So he asked Elizabeth several questions that may have seemed a little odd but were vital to Chip and Whittemore.

"Do you remember what day it was?"

Professor Baker answered for Elizabeth. "I remember very well," he said wryly. "It was Tuesday, August fourteenth. Beth was twelve years old. That was nine long years ago."

"Where was the cottage located?" Chip asked. "Weren't there any other houses nearby?"

"Only one, at that time," Professor Baker said. "A big gray house with a black roof sitting some distance back from the beach. I remember it well, because it was the only house surrounded by trees along the beach. They must have been cultivated in a special soil because the house itself was surrounded by sand."

"Didn't the boy hear you?" Chip persisted. "Did you ever see him again or learn his name?"

Elizabeth shook her head, "No, he didn't give any sign at all that he heard me. The waves were carrying me high in the air and then down into the hollows, and each time I reached the crest I could see him. I watched him walk all the way to the big house, but he never once looked in my direction. It was a terrible feeling to know that help was so close and yet so far away. I never saw him again and never knew his name."

ELIZABETH'S STORY

A short time later, Chip and Whittemore left and started back to Jeff. Not a word was spoken on the way. When they reached the big dorm, Chip went directly to his room and cautiously turned on his desk light to read Whitty's note. Whitty had been only twelve years old when the incident occurred, and he, too, was a weak swimmer. It was a wonder he hadn't gotten in trouble himself. He could never have gotten Elizabeth to shore, even if he had tried. Chip read Whitty's note again. A change of a word here or there, and it might well have been written by Elizabeth.

Chip tiptoed out of the room, knocked on Whittemore's door, and entered. Whitty was pacing restlessly back and forth, but he stopped when Chip handed him the note.

"Here's the note, Whitty," Chip said gently. "Why not burn it right now, destroy it, and everything connected with it?"

Whittemore got a match from his desk, lighted the paper, and placed it in the metal waste basket. The two boys stood motionless until the piece of paper was just black, brittle particles. Whitty leaned over then and slowly ground the ashes with his fingertips.

"Practice tomorrow?" Chip asked softly.

Whittemore took a deep breath and smiled for the first time in weeks. It was a bright smile of gratitude, and he took a long time answering. Then he nodded, "You got it!"

Whitty touched the charred particles again with the tips of his fingers. "I wish I could say all the things I want to say, Chip, but I can't find the words. I wasn't very strong then, and I had just learned to swim. Besides, I had been warned about the ocean, and I was scared. I heard Elizabeth scream, all right, but she was being carried out to sea, and I was sure she would be drowned.

"I knew I wasn't strong enough to help her, and I was afraid I would be carried out to sea too. Her screams grew fainter and fainter, and I turned and swam to shore to get help. But when I reached the shore, I didn't hear her cries anymore, and I went on up to the house and never said anything to anyone. I never said anything to anyone until I told you."

Chip softly remarked, "Well, I know somebody in the psychology department who'd be willing to listen if you want to talk to her." Whittemore paused and resumed his pacing. Chip said nothing more, realizing it was best for Whitty if he could talk it out of his heart and soul and memory.

"We were leaving that day, and I couldn't wait to get away. I've been trying to run away from it ever since. But no matter where I went or what I did, those terrified screams followed. And ever since then, whenever an accident or emergency occurred, I've stood there helplessly, bound by a chain of fear I couldn't break.

"Somehow or other, I got to be a good swimmer and an expert sailor during my years at Camp All-America, but I never lost the fear nor forgot the screams of the drowning girl. I think now they are gone for good.

"I wish I could better express my thanks. But I guess about all you want to know is that those ashes have ended all the faking and showboating and loafing and quitting—forever!"

CHAPTER 20

Ten Seconds to Play!

PHILIP WHITTEMORE showed up for practice Friday afternoon, surprising most of the players and all of the coaching staff. That was only part of the surprise. For the first time, Whitty really cut loose, and it was a revelation even to his most bitter critics. He tore through his tackles, and in the sprints he ran as though it was a life-or-death race. Many of the players winked and attributed Whittemore's new look to a last-minute desire to atone for Tuesday's debacle, a last-ditch effort to showboat his way back to a starting position. But Chip's friends, knowing Whittemore a little better than the others, realized this time it was for keeps.

Coach Ralston gave the players a last-minute pep talk and sent them to the showers. Afterward, Chip, Soapy, and Whittemore hurried downtown to Grayson's, where some important people were waiting.

One of Chip's best camp assistants was there along with his brother and mom and five of the nicest men

Chip had ever met. Jimmie Dodd rushed to Chip as soon as he entered the door, and the others crowded around Chip and Whittemore, shaking their hands as if they hadn't seen them for five years instead of five weeks.

Jimmie kept right on talking, giving Chip a complete report. "I made the team, Chip," he said, winking triumphantly. "And guess what? Dad says I'm better than Frankie was when he was in middle school. Quarterback! Here, look at this! Good fake, right?"

And the Camp All-America crowd was waiting at the players' entrance when State trotted out on the field. "Go get 'em, Chip!"

"Snare those passes, Whitty!"

"We're with you, guys! Hit 'em hard!"

Chip's heart was pumping as the crowd roar seemed to engulf him. It was in his eyes and ears and lungs, and every time he took a long, awed look at all the spectators, his blood turned to ice, and he started shaking all over from the top of his head to the tips of his toes.

Then during the warm-up wind sprints, bending, twisting, zipping the passes, and booting the ball, some of the stress disappeared.

The bands were blasting away, taking turns playing tunes Chip couldn't name, and the fans were yelling their approval of Coach Curly Ralston's new team.

Captain Mike Brennan joined the Tech captain, the referee, umpire, field judge and head linesman at the fifty-yard line, and then Mike came hustling back to the bench, shouting, "We receive! South goal!" Chip came into the circle around the coach, joined in the team clasp, and was on his way—starting as State's varsity quarterback.

Standing on the five-yard line, Chip's heart beat fast and high in his chest during the eternity of waiting. And it stuck there, thumping loud in his ears while the strength drained out of his arms and knees. The crowd noise seemed to die away then, and the blurred figures of the men in the white caps, striped shirts, and white knickers seemed to get smaller and farther away. The shakes started again, and just when it seemed he couldn't stand the pent-up tension another second, the referee's whistle blasted away his trance. The game was on!

Chip charged forward clear past the ten-yard line before he realized the distance of the kick. Then he backtracked frantically as the ball tumbled end over end, over the goal line, and into the end zone. It was State's ball, first and ten on the twenty, and the huge crowd was on its feet. State came out of the huddle fast, and Finley drove into the line at full speed, picking up four yards. Chip used him again, and the blockbuster was good for four more, making it third and two on the State twenty-eight.

Chip sent Finley into the line again and seemingly plunked the ball into his belly before he turned and faked to Ace Gibbons cutting across to the left side of the line. There was confusion in the Tech line and in the stands. Where was the ball?

Before anyone could answer that question, Chip straightened up and fired to Larry Higgins cutting down the right sideline. There were three of them up in the air for the ball: two Tech backs and Larry. But Larry brought it down on the forty and carried the two defenders for another five yards on his back.

Up in the broadcasting booth, Gee-Gee Gray was talking to several million people, describing the game of the week. "State is using the split-T formation with a flanker on the right. Higgins pulled in that pass. The big end is six-five and one of the two seniors on Curly Ralston's surprise team.

"First and ten. The ball is resting on the State forty-five. State is out of the huddle now, ends split. Number 40—right halfback—is the flanker out to the right. It's a split buck with Finley carrying across the fifty to the Tech forty-eight. There's a gain of seven yards. Finley is State's sophomore fullback sensation.

"Hold on, there's a marker on the play. It may be an offside here. Yes, offside on number 60. That one's on Tiny Tim McCarthy, the left guard. He's the other senior starting on this team. A five-yard penalty and that makes it first and fifteen with the ball on the State forty. Number 44, that's Chip Hilton, State's new quarterback wizard, the player you've been reading so much about, fakes beautifully. He's back for a pass—he's rushed—he can't get the pass away—he's running to the right. He's going to pass—he gets a long one away.

"Speed Morris, State's new left halfback, is behind the defense—has the ball—may go all the way. He's on the thirty, the twenty-five, and oh! He's hit hard on the twenty and downed. Make it the eighteen-yard line, and that's a good one. They won't call that one back. That pass by Hilton was a beauty. Hilton set that up by faking to Finley and hitting Morris coming out of the backfield with the pass.

"What a combination these two sophomores make. Finley busting the line and drawing in the opponent's defense and Hilton with his amazing faking to Finley and finding his pass receivers behind the tight defense.

"First and ten now. There's a back in motion—it's a pitchout to Gibbons—good old Ace has the ball, and he's hit. He laterals to 44—Hilton has the ball now, and he's going to score! He's in for six points! State scores! That was a beautiful play. Hilton to Gibbons on a pitchout, and then when Ace was stopped, he lateraled to Hilton, who went all the way. No sophomoritis with this one. Hilton will kick as Morris spots the ball down. It's a nice snap from Mike Brennan, team captain. Hilton kicks, and it's good! State leads, 7- 0."

It was touch and go the first half, but State went to the locker room leading 14-7. Chip whispered a few words to Rockwell just before the Statesmen came back on the field, and the veteran coach nodded.

State started off the second half as though it meant to run Tech off the field. Chip clicked on seven of nine passes to bring the ball to the Tech fifteen. Tech stiffened then, and Chip connected on a perfect placekick to make the score State 17, Tech 7.

Most teams let down a bit after they have traveled the length of the field to score, and State was no exception. The ten-point margin looked big. Tech was set to receive, and Chip's kick was gathered in by the visitors' brilliant return specialist on the five-yard line.

The speedy runner angled for the left sideline, picking up a wall of blockers. Just when it looked as if he was trapped near the sideline, he turned and passed across and back down the field to his waiting teammate. This player had pulled a perfect fake; he had thrown a roll block at one of State's charging tacklers, struggled slowly to his feet, and appeared to limp upfield. Gathering in the lateral on his twenty-yard line, he sped up the opposite side of the field.

Biggie Cohen had been sucked into the wedge, and Wally Curtis had failed to protect the flank in his eagerness to get into the action. Their side of the field was wide open, and the Tech runner sped up the right sideline, heading for a sure touchdown. Speed Morris, playing safety on the kickoff, had been drawn over to the right and was out of the play.

Chip had been dumped hard on the forty-yard line and got to his feet just in time to see the play develop. He turned and dashed straight back toward his own goal, sprinting for the far corner of the field. The crowd noise from the stands was deafening as the fans watched the desperate race. Chip was at a slight distance disadvantage, but his long legs ate up the yardage, and he gradually forged ahead.

In a beautiful dive tackle he brought the ball carrier down. It was first down and goal to go for Tech on the State seven-yard line. The home stands roared in relief, and it was all for Chip.

Mike Brennan called for a time-out, and Coach Ralston sent Schwartz in for Higgins and Anderson for McCarthy. Then State gave the home fans something to cheer about; the Statesmen dug in and took the ball away from Tech on downs.

Tech returned the favor, holding State to no gain on three successive plays. When Chip went back to punt, the ball was resting on the one-foot line, and he was only a half step away from the dangerous end-zone line. But he got the ball away in a low, twisting kick that angled for the right sideline and out-of-bounds on the fifty-yard stripe. It was a beautiful clutch kick.

Tech couldn't gain an inch and punted out-of-bounds on the State five-yard line. State couldn't run it out, and Chip wasn't ready to gamble and risk an interception. So Chip punted again, and the ball was in the air and Tech was signaling for a fair catch when the quarter ended. It was Tech's ball on its own forty-eight-yard line.

On the first play of the fourth quarter, the Tech quarterback winged a long pass down the center of the field.

Both ends converged on Chip, but he cut in front of them at the last instant and snared the ball on the twelve-yard line. The Tech center dropped Chip with a vicious tackle just as he caught the ball. Chip still wasn't ready to risk a passing play. And when three running plays lost five yards, it was fourth down with the ball resting on the seven-yard line. Chip dropped back in the end zone, and Tech shifted into an eight-man defensive line. Tech was after the ball!

Surprisingly, State's line suddenly seemed full of holes. The Tech linemen barged through at full speed, almost reaching Chip with the ball. Then Chip shocked everybody in the stadium except the State players. He pivoted and ran along the end-zone line, barely evading the charging Tech rushers. The field ahead of him was filled with State blockers, and Chip broke out in the open. He got up to the State thirty-five before the Tech safety knocked him out-of-bounds.

Chip's teammates were as happy as the State fans. But all went for nothing on the very next play. Chip faked to Finley and gave the ball to Gibbons. Ace broke through right tackle and, for one brief second, was away. Then he was hit by two of the Tech linebackers with a crash heard all over the stadium, and the ball popped out of his usually sure senior hands. The great State cheer that had greeted the breakaway turned to a groan.

Tech recovered Gibbons's fumble on its own forty and electrified the huge crowd by scoring on the first play with a long pass into the end zone. The kick was good, and the score was now State 17, Tech 14.

State received and worked the ball to their own forty when Gibbons fumbled again. Tech recovered on the State forty-two. The Tech quarterback showed why he was an all-American the previous year by fooling the

State rushers with his "hidden-ball" trickery, and the Tech left halfback sped through a big hole in the line and down to the State twelve before Chip nailed him.

On the next play he passed to his tall right end, who leaped high above Morris to pull in the ball in the end zone. Tech led 20-17. The State fans began to roar then, and when the Tech quarterback sent the ball spinning between the uprights, it was one solid thundering sound. The extra point attempt was good, and the score was Tech 21, State 17.

Just as State was getting ready to receive, Chip looked over to the bench and nodded to Rockwell. Rock said something to Ralston, and Whittemore came tearing out on the field to replace Wally Curtis.

The kick shot high and directly at Chip. He swerved sharply and headed up the right sideline. Then Whittemore earned a terrific cheer from the stands by cutting down two would-be tacklers with a tremendous block, and Chip carried the ball all the way to the State forty.

Eddie Anderson was injured on the play, and Tiny Tim McCarthy hustled out on the field. "C'mon, guys!" he cried. "It's now or never! Give it to 'em, Chip!"

Chip tried and his teammates tried, but Tech was fighting just as valiantly. On fourth down and three yards to go, Chip glanced despairingly at the clock and reluctantly dropped back to kick. The Tech forward line didn't rush him with abandon this time; instead, the ends advanced cautiously across the line of scrimmage, and the guards and tackles charged straight ahead, each protecting his own territory. Chip angled the ball out of bounds on the Tech ten-yard line. The visitors' quarterback was playing it smart, using up every precious second and running out the clock.

TEN SECONDS TO PLAY!

On fourth down and five yards to go, there were four minutes left to play, and Tech had the ball on the State forty-yard line. The tension had mounted with each deliberate move of the Tech quarterback, and now it was almost at the breaking point. Tech called time, and Brennan herded State into a huddle.

"This is our last chance, guys," Mike said grimly. "They've got to punt now. Let's give Chip some good blocking when he gets the ball. Good, hard blocks, got it?"

When time was in, the Tech quarterback kept at it, dropping leisurely back into punting position and cleverly booting the ball out-of-bounds on the State fifteen-yard line. He made sure there was no chance for a State return.

Chip knew Tech was expecting him to pass, so he faked to Morris driving into the line, carried the ball himself for three quick strides, and then used a shovel-pass pitch out to Finley. Fireball continued on as if to circle right end. Then, just when it seemed he was going to be thrown for a big loss by a swarm of Tech tacklers, he stabbed his foot in the ground and fired the ball, as though it were a baseball, straight to Red Schwartz at midfield. Schwartz was hit almost as soon as he button-hooked, but he held the ball. The pass was good for thirty-eight yards and made it first and ten on the Tech forty-seven-yard line. The visitors called time.

In the huddle, Chip looked around the circle of faces. Red Schwartz, Speed Morris, Biggie Cohen, and Soapy Smith were eyeing him with alert expressions, and shoulder to shoulder with them were Fireball Finley, Philip Whittemore, Silent Joe Maxim, Mike Brennan, Ace Gibbons, and Tiny Tim McCarthy. The team waited in silence for Chip to call the play and to make the decisions. His teammates' resolute attitudes expressed their confidence in Chip's leadership.

TEN SECONDS TO PLAY!

"Well, it doesn't get any better than this! Time is running out, guys," Chip said slowly. "We'll run the plays from formation on the ball." He turned to Whittemore. "All right, Whitty," he said pointedly, "this is what you've been waiting for. It's up to you! Let's go!"

Tech didn't know anything about Whittemore but soon found out. Chip hit him with a fast timing pass over the line, which was good for six. Then he passed to him out in the flat. Then right over the middle again. Then again. That was enough for the Tech captain. He called time with the ball on the Tech thirty-two and a minute and five seconds left to play.

When time was in, Chip promptly passed to Whittemore over the line, and it was good for another first down on the Tech twenty. The Tech secondary tackled Whitty viciously on that one, trying to wrestle the ball out of his hands. But Whitty held the precious cargo desperately, clutching the ball as if it was pure gold. Chip called an audible at the line and sent Morris into the line for no gain. Precious seconds ticked off the scoreboard clock.

There were only ten desperate seconds left to play when Chip faked a pass downfield to Schwartz, while Whittemore delayed for a count of three, and then faked another to Morris. Then Whitty swung around behind Chip and took the ball out of his hand and circled right end. Chip held his pose, arm in the air, watching Whittemore's progress. This was it! It meant a good start for State and Whittemore and Ralston and Biggie and Red and Soapy and Speed and for all of his own hopes, or it meant disaster!

Whitty was hit half a dozen times on that run. And while he was battling, fighting, scrambling, and twisting toward the goal, the clock ran out. But he kept going, staggering forward under the weight of the three Tech players he carried on his back, until he reached and fell across the goal line to put State ahead 23-21.

The game was over, and Whittemore had won it! He was still dazed and half unconscious when the official informed the team captain, Mike Brennan, that the extra-point try was not necessary. Final score: State 23, Tech 21!

The State bench and the players on the field charged Whitty then and lifted him up in the air. Chip was one of those who held him up there and cheered while unashamed tears streamed down Whittemore's face. But Whitty didn't forget Chip in his moment of glory. He reached down and grasped his new friend's hand, gripping it thankfully, expressing, in the only way he could, his heartfelt gratitude.

State's fans were all around them, mobbing the field in a frenzy of joy. And one of the wildest and most joyous shrieks was contributed by a girl who nine years ago had screamed in terror as she was being carried out to sea. No one had heard her then, and no one heard her now. But life was going to be happier for a boy named Philip Whittemore.

Curly Ralston, Henry Rockwell, and Nik Nelson sat in the head coach's office and replayed that last-second victory a dozen times after the game. Then the talk swung around to that memorable midnight session at Camp Sundown when Ralston had announced he was breaking up his veteran team.

"What induced you to make that decision, Curly?" Rockwell asked. "You never did tell us."

"It must have been Hilton's playing," Nelson said. "He was the whole show for my money."

"It was partly his playing," Ralston conceded, "but mostly something else. Rock, do you know what?"

Rockwell shook his head, "I don't believe I know, Curly. I thought Chip looked good all along. Western was the first test because they are a first-class team, probably one of the top preseason picks in the country. Chip gave them a rough time."

Ralston nodded, "He did that, all right. But it wasn't so much his playing as something else. Don't get me wrong! I thought he was sensational from the beginning. He certainly sold Mike Brennan.

"Right after Schwartz scored in that game, if you remember, Mike slapped Chip on the back and made a fuss over him. First time I ever saw Mike do that to anyone. Mike's hard and tough to the core and not given to emotional displays. But he told me more by his actions toward Chip than he could have with a thousand words. And he told the rest of the veterans. That was what I was waiting for. You see, Mike and Tims Lansing are roommates and close friends. Hilton had to be something special to win Mike away from Tims.

"I liked the playing of Hilton, Finley, Morris, and that clown Smith enough to make them starters, but that's still not the reason I made the decision."

There was a pause as they all laughed and remembered Soapy bursting into their cabin the first night at Camp Sundown. Then the conversation turned serious again.

"You've got me," Nelson admitted.

"I'm surprised," Ralston said lightly. "Maybe I ought to review a few things, recall a few incidents to mind.

"Remember the intrasquad scrimmage? Remember the lateral Whittemore threw to Hilton? Of course you do. Remember my congratulations to Whittemore and

Hilton? Well, Whittemore didn't deserve any credit whatsoever. I knew that all the time. He was scared silly, completely demoralized, and trying to avoid being tackled.

"Hilton covered up for him; he called for the ball and made the play. I liked that—I liked it when Hilton took Morris's defensive halfback position and steamed Cohen and Finley up to such a point that they nearly tore the vets apart. Remember, Rock? I thought you would. Hilton did that to cover up Whittemore's defensive weakness. You were puzzled by that at first, Rock, but you figured it out, too, didn't you? Of course you did! I knew you did at the time.

"I liked it when Hilton took Morris's defensive position against Western. And I especially liked Hilton's astuteness when he was back with Morris in the 6-3-2 that afternoon. He maneuvered Morris into taking a punt he should have taken himself, and then he threw a wonderful block so that Morris could impress me with his open-field running and account for Morris's move to the safety position and his own move to defensive left halfback. Again, that was a part of his plan to help Whittemore."

Ralston caught Rockwell's glance and grinned. "A player with that kind of football astuteness and skill comes along once in a lifetime. He has to be recognized and his talents developed. Hilton can do more things on a football field than anyone I ever coached. But it was his football intelligence and ability to make split-second decisions that convinced me he could become the greatest quarterback in college football.

"Now to get back to Whittemore and Hilton's evident desire to help him make good. I can't tell you the why of that one. I can't figure it out to save my neck. Perhaps it will show up in the results of a lot of games yet to be won before the decision justifies itself.

"But watching Whittemore today, watching him block and fight and bull his way for that winning touchdown, convinced me that Chip Hilton knows a lot more about what makes boys tick than we do.

"I have no idea what transformed Whittemore from a terrible football player on Tuesday to a star this afternoon. But I know Chip Hilton was the guiding genius."

He turned to Rockwell. "When you told me Chip wanted Whittemore in the game, that he had that much confidence in him, I was a little dubious. But I knew Chip wouldn't trifle in a situation that desperate, and I didn't hesitate.

"Well, we can be thankful we relied on Chip's judgment and stuck with him. He saw something inside Whittemore we would never have recognized. I know that Chip helped Whittemore win some kind of personal inner battle, and whatever it was, it gave us a great end and a team that hasn't a single weakness as far as I can see.

"And it's all because of Chip Hilton—all because of his unswerving loyalty, courage, and belief in another boy."

• • •

CHIP HILTON and his teammates playing for State football are riding high after their opening victory. Coach Curly Ralston's reliance on the sophomores is paying off, and it continues to pay off until the crucial game against A & M. The conference title is at stake. Then State's hopes are suddenly shattered as Chip and his sophomore crew are suspended for violating the curfew rule! This exciting story reaches its thrilling climax on the day of the A & M game.

Be sure you catch *Fourth-Down Showdown*, as Coach Clair Bee's exciting sports series continues.

Afterword

I REMEMBER the phone call like it was yesterday. "Chuck, this is Clair Bee calling, and I'd like you to come work at Kutsher's Sports Academy. Are you interested?"

Interested! I'd heard about Kutsher's for years. It was the place to be for New York area basketball players, and the chance to work there was not to be taken lightly. More important to me, however, was the fact that Clair Bee himself was calling me. Having read the Chip Hilton sports books growing up, I knew who Clair Bee was more as an author than as a great coach. As a young and still pretty naïve nineteen-year-old, I was enchanted by the opportunity to be associated with Coach Bee and the Kutsher camp program.

So I jumped at the chance to work at Kutsher's, right?

As much as I wanted to, I just couldn't do it. I had already accepted a summer job working as a lifeguard at one of the local beach clubs, and I felt that I'd made a commitment and it just wouldn't be right to break it now that a better offer had come along. I've often wondered what that summer experience at Kutsher's would have been like, but I've never wondered about the correctness of my decision. It was the kind of decision that Chip Hilton would have made, and Coach Rockwell would certainly have understood it.

Many years have passed since that time back in the late 1960s, and yet the values that Chip Hilton found dear have remained a part of my own life. In the time I've spent working with young athletes and others, I've continually helped myself through difficult circumstances by asking myself, "Now, what would Chip Hilton do in this situation?" Wrestling with this simple question has on many occasions led me down the road to the right answer.

Now that the Chip Hilton sports books are being updated and published for a new generation of readers, I intend to do what I can to introduce Chip, his friends, and Coach Rockwell to the athletes, parents, coaches, and others in the American swimming community. The stories are precious and the lessons are timeless.

Welcome back, Chip Hilton!

CHUCK WIELGUS
Executive Director,
USA Swimming

Your Score Card

I have   I expect
read: to read:

_____ _____   1. *Touchdown Pass:* The first story in the
series, introducing you to William "Chip"
Hilton and all his friends at Valley Falls High
during an exciting football season.

_____ _____   2. *Championship Ball:* With a broken
ankle and an unquenchable spirit, Chip
wins the state basketball championship and
an even greater victory over himself.

_____ _____   3. *Strike Three!* In the hour of his team's
greatest need, Chip Hilton takes to the
mound and puts the Big Reds in line for all-
state honors.

_____ _____   4. *Clutch Hitter!* Chip's summer job at
Mansfield Steel Company gives him a chance
to play baseball on the famous Steeler team
where he uses his head as well as his war club.

_____ _____   5. *A Pass and a Prayer:* Chip's last football
season is a real challenge as conditions for
the Big Reds deteriorate. Somehow he must
keep the team together for their coach.

_____ _____   6. *Hoop Crazy:* When three-point fever
spreads to the Valley Falls basketball varsity, Chip Hilton has to do something, and
fast!

YOUR SCORE CARD

I have   I expect
read: to read:

About the Author

CLAIR BEE, who coached football, baseball, and basketball at the collegiate level, is considered one of the greatest basketball coaches of all time—both collegiate and professional. His winning percentage, 82.6, ranks first overall among any major college coaches, past or present. His name lives on forever in numerous halls of fame. The Coach Clair Bee and Chip Hilton awards are presented annually at the Basketball Hall of Fame honoring college coaches and players for their commitment to education, personal character, and service to others on and off the court. He is the author of the twenty-four-volume, bestselling Chip Hilton Sports series, which has influenced many sports and literary notables, including best-selling author John Grisham.